Thief of Lives

Also by Kit Reed

THIEF
OF
LIVES

Stories by
Kit Reed

UNIVERSITY OF MISSOURI PRESS
Columbia and London

Copyright © 1992 by Kit Reed
University of Missouri Press, Columbia, Missouri 65201
Printed and bound in the United States of America
All rights reserved

5 4 3 2 1   96 95 94 93 92

Library of Congress Cataloging-in-Publication Data

Reed, Kit.
    Thief of lives : stories / by Kit Reed.
       p.   cm.
    ISBN 0-8262-0850-9 (alk. paper)
    I. Title
PS3568.E367T48   1992
813' .54—dc20   92-20699
                                          CIP

⊗™ This paper meets the minimum requirements of
the American National Standard for Permanence of Paper
for Printed Library Materials, Z39.48, 1984.

Some of the stories in this volume first appeared in the following journals:
"In the *Squalus*," "Mr. Rabbit," and "Thing of Snow" in *Transatlantic Review*;
"Journey to the Center of the Earth" in *Voice Literary Supplement*; "The Pro-
tective Pessimist" in *Texas Review*; "The Garden Club" and "Fourth of July"
in *Chronicles*; "The Jonahs" and "Prisoner of War" in *Tampa Review*.
"Winter" was first published in *Winter's Tales 15* (Macmillan, 1969) and
in *Argosy* in London; it was also selected for the *Norton Anthology of
Contemporary Literature* (1987).

Designer: Kristie Lee
Typesetter: Connell Zeko Type and Graphics
Printer: Thomson-Shore, Inc.
Binder: Thomson-Shore, Inc.
Typefaces: Palatino and Optima

Not the first or the last short story
collection to be dedicated to

George P. Garrett, with love

Contents

Thief of Lives

In the *Squalus*

He was under water for too long; lying in the shell of the submarine for more than thirty hours, he left his body and his living mates and became at one with the dead floating on the other side of the bulkhead. In the last seconds before the lights failed a few men had scrambled into the control room to join the living; Larkin and the others in the bow let them through and then, facing the rushing ocean, they were forced to close the door against the rest, so that there were twenty-six dead sealed in the flooded engine room. The survivors lay together under the great weight of the ocean, Larkin alive with the rest but already cut adrift from them.

If he was waiting for rescue he was not aware of it; he heard only vaguely the SOS the others tapped out on the metal hull. When he took his own turn he was not aware he did so and he was not listening for a reply. Instead he imagined he heard the voices of the dead reverberating in the metal; he heard the dead in his own ship, in all the drowned ships of all time in growing volume, making a remote but ceaseless boom against the hull.

As a child Larkin had looked out across flat New Mexico and dreamed of water. In all those dusty summers he prepared his eyes for the ocean, superimposing that great, watery horizon on the desert. With other landlocked boys he would choose the Navy, going to sea with a thirst he did not yet understand. Married, he would take Marylee and their little girl for vacations at one beach after another, lifting his daughter high above the water and bringing her down quickly, so they would both laugh at the shining splash. He may have been certain he would die by drowning, that in the end he would let the water take him; he would be muffled and shrouded by water; water would carry away all his doubt and pain so that in the end there would be nothing left but water, washing over his own skull's bright, eternal grin.

Instead Alvah Larkin found himself safe in the *Squalus*, freezing in the dark. It was only a matter of time before the diving bell clanked against the hull and he would have to begin the tortuous escape. It would kill them if I stayed here, he thought in the last minutes before he gave himself to darkness. Janny, he thought, seeing the child and Marylee arrested in attitudes of waiting: on the rocks looking out to sea, pleading at the main gate of the base, poised, white-faced on the dock. They would always look to the horizon; Marylee would not let the girl look down, into the water. If Larkin stayed where he was they would remain fixed like that forever; still death seduced him and for some hours it seemed as though he would not have to go back. Numbed, he was able to lose track of time and project eternity.

In the last freezing hours he may have thought he had seen Jonah, or had been Jonah, or was that the face of Christ hovering just beyond the lights streaking his closed eyelids? There was a clang on the hull, the bell, and so he would not find out this time. Instead he had to pull himself back and join the others. When the hatch opened to let them into the bell he would hesitate only a second before going, blinking, into an uncertain birth.

In the bell he heard himself saying, "Yeah, I'll be glad to get back to the wife and kid."

When they were all safe in sick bay, President Roosevelt talked to them; his voice was full of static but sad, expressing national relief. Everybody was going right back into submarines, they told the president; Larkin wanted to get back on duty as soon as possible but he knew it wouldn't make any difference; it was too late. He could see in Marylee's eyes that it was too late.

"Oh Alvah," she said. "Those poor men."

Janny hugged him hard. "Daddy, you were gone too long."

He buried his face in her. "But I came back."

Marylee said firmly, "Daddy always comes back."

So he put Janny down and kissed his wife, understanding as she shrank for a split second that he was surrounded by the dead of the *Squalus,* he would walk with the twenty-six drowned men at his back for the rest of his life; even as Marylee threw herself on him in all her warmth, murmuring and pretending nothing had changed, he knew how cold his touch must seem to her, cold as the touch of Lazarus; he had been to death and back and it separated them. Without ever talking about it he had been preparing Marylee for years; he had chosen the Navy, he was no better than anybody else and so one day he would probably be lost at sea. She'd never admitted she understood what he was trying to tell her; after all, submarines were safer than surface ships, there was no war, he was Alvah, not just anybody. She had changed in the hours he was entombed in the *Squalus.* Comprehending, she had accepted; she may even have known that it would be easier for both of them if he hadn't come back up. She could stop pretending she wasn't afraid for him. She would never have to lose him again; instead she could grow old with the memory of a husband perpetually in his early thirties, always smiling and sure; returned, he saw all this in her eyes.

In the car going home from the base he said, "Do you still want your new baby?" Marylee kept her eyes on the road but he thought she said "Yes" and he said with urgency, "Then let's have your baby."

It didn't keep the drowned ship out of their bed. She had to know why he was always cold and anxious and couldn't sleep. He put his face close and tried to tell her everything: how the skipper had kept them quiet and organized after they closed the last watertight door; how they were put on watches, keeping order in the timeless chaos of the dark; why the skipper could not let anybody mention their shipmates, trapped a few inches away, any more than he could let them contemplate the ocean, separated from them only by the metal hull. His dead shipmates.

He was trembling in the dark bedroom. "But they were there."

"You heard them pounding and calling."

"Nobody heard them. They were all dead."

She tried to comfort him. "Then there was nothing you could do. There was nothing anybody could do."

He turned away from her. *But I knew they were there.* How could he explain?

Marylee filled the house with friends, trying to crowd out the dead. She was pregnant again; she would fill the house with his children, sending them clattering into his silence to diffuse his memories. But he knew they were still there, and the knowledge marked him. Even after the boat was raised and the bodies were taken out and returned to their families, they were still in the *Squalus* for Larkin; even after the salvaged boat was renamed and recommissioned, the twenty-six men were in the *Squalus* and the *Squalus* lay in the dark waters off Portsmouth, so that whenever Larkin met another of the survivors they got too drunk and talked too much, neither listening to the other but talking because they had to; together they had to shut them out.

It was important that he stay in subs. After Pearl Harbor he would take command of his own S-boat; immuring himself in the close air and the smell of heavily oiled machinery, he would dive and look for them. During the war he managed each patrol according to the book, performing perfectly; he was aggressive and cautious in appropriate measure, never jeopardizing his crew. Nobody aboard could know that once he was alone in his cubicle he would sit on the edge of his bunk, pale and sweating in his khakis, and drop his head into his two hands and draw within himself and listen, offering his own life and theirs too, if necessary, for the lives of those who were already lost. Toward the end of the war he would begin to drink too much, beginning another kind of immersion.

At home the summer after the bell brought him to the surface, he would take Janny down on the rocks by the water and sit while she played. Because he knew she wasn't listening, he talked about all of it, and when she said nothing in response he was able to imagine that she understood everything he told her.

"I had to come back."

"Daddy, look at the bird."

"I had to come back for you and Mommy, I had to keep faith. Does that make any sense to you?"

He imagined that she turned to him, saying, *Daddy, you had to come back for us. Otherwise we would have died.*

That's what I thought.

We were waiting and waiting.

I knew you were. That's why I had to come.

There was nothing else you could have done.

He said, "It was for you."

"What, Daddy?" She had disorderly curls and her freckled skin was so white that he could see the blue veins running underneath; she was too beautiful to have come from him and Marylee, she was their hope.

"I said, come here and let me tuck in your shirt."

As it turned out it was she who was faithless; Janny fell through the ice and drowned on the longest night of that winter. Larkin went out to look for her in the deep midnight pitch of five P.M., and in the swirl of dank air knew he had never left the *Squalus.* Marylee was with him, already sobbing; when she stumbled he grabbed her arm and caught her up but his gloves were thick and his fingers cold and even though he saw them closed around her arm, he felt nothing. After a while the police found them and took them home; somebody had located Janny finally by the bookbag frozen to the ice next to the black hole she had made, plunging through. Now they would break the news to the Larkins, setting them down in the midst of arrangements, the first sympathy calls, visitors leaving them each with a firm push that meant: *continue.* If Larkin had known, trapped in the *Squalus,* that this would happen, he would have offered his life for her, but when he thought about it he would always wonder if instead, in some occult foreknowledge, he had offered her life for his, whether he had in some way sent the child down to look for the others, if not to redeem them then to join them in some pledge of his own faith and ceaseless grief.

When the rituals were over and her tears were finished at last

Marylee put her head against him, saying, "She told me she would be at Dorothy's. If I had only checked."

"She *was* there, right up to the last minute," he said, and then he went on with the formula which would make it possible for her to keep on living; he went on even though he was not convinced of it. "There was nothing anybody could have done."

It will be enough for her, he thought. She has the baby. He was ready to let go but Marylee saw him drifting and reached out.

"Alvah." She had him by the hand and she was looking sharply into his face. "Alvah, I'm going to need you."

He answered automatically. "I'm right here." He could feel the increasing pressure; he had a choice; he would not look at her.

She let go. "I'll always love you anyway."

He said, without answering, "I'll be right here."

The baby was to be born in March, and Marylee would pin her life to it. Larkin would give her three more children to replace the dead one, leaving her almost satisfied, but the new ones were nothing of his; they would swirl around him without realizing how remote their father was because they had never known anything else. Only the dead child was really his, and he would spend most of his life with her and the others; he had been there once and he belonged with them; he would go down in dive after dive to look for them. When he was no longer in submarines he would swim, going fierce, dogged, unremitting lengths in the base pool.

He kept a picture of Janny on his desk wherever he went but never looked at it; instead he would withdraw into himself and rehearse the afternoons they'd spent together on the rocks. He would feel her in his arms, angular and smelling a little, because all living children smell; he'd imagine her on the dock, flinging herself on him again and again. He belonged with Janny and the others; he belonged with all his classmates who had died at Pearl or in the Coral Sea and he imagined that eventually he would join the child and all the others would surround them: tableau. He could not think beyond that moment, but imagined peace. All this seemed more real to him than his wife or his living children, whom he would kiss abstractedly, so that he remained a solitary in the busy house Marylee kept in an attempt to lure him back to life.

By the end of the war Larkin was drinking too much and his men knew it; eventually his superiors became aware of it. They put him on shore duty so they could keep an eye on him; they sent him to sea where he wouldn't have so many opportunities; they put him in a Navy hospital in an attempt to dry him out; eventually they had to survey him, so that in his forties he was retired for medical reasons, living in New London because he couldn't leave the water or the rocks or any of the rest of it; he used to take his tackle and go fishing off a point where he could watch the base. Once that first winter of his retirement he took his tackle and walked to the center of the bridge that spanned the Thames, looking for a long time at the black surface of the water. If he jumped it would be over in a minute, but first he would have to go through the awkward business of getting rid of his tackle box and making it over the guardrail, or if he hung on to the box because it would make it quicker, then he would have a hard time getting over the rail at all. The problem could have been solved, but he was held back not so much by the weight of his clothes, his boots, his accoutrements as by the fact of Marylee; he owed her something, if only freedom from another vigil by the water, another funeral. Instead he went to his usual place and fished, finishing the fifth of rye from his tackle box, so blurring the days that it was months before he thought about what he had almost done. Looking over at Marylee at dinner one night, he could not be sure whether he was grateful or resented her because he was still there. He went out to a bar and was gone overnight. Marylee greeted him late the next day; she was pale and taut but she didn't say anything. He was still working at part-time jobs in this period, trying to stave off his desperate boredom, but none of them lasted for long. After a while there weren't any more jobs; he and Marylee both marked it, but neither of them would say anything.

As he moved into his fifties, Larkin would go off for days at a time, disappearing on desperate binges. He would always mark the first time, not because of any place he went or any thing he did but because of Marylee, who came for him and found him. He came to in somebody's back room to find her leaning over him. There were two policemen with her; they made him understand they had been looking for him for a week, they'd been about to drag the river, but the words had no particular meaning; the only meaning he saw was in Marylee's face. For the first time he was aware of all the accumulated pain and fatigue of several years; he saw with regret how much he had aged her. He reached out, longing to make everything all right for her and for his living children, but he was appalled by the changes life had made in all of them. Only Janny remained unchanged, with her face forever bright.

After that he was able to trace the progress of his life by the lines in his wife's face, by the looks of reproach in the faces of his growing children; he marked it by the aches in his own bones and his compounded boredom and loneliness, the pain which would not be drowned in rye, and in his periodic attempts to stop drinking he would thank God that he was getting older, knowing that eventually time would put an end to this—it was the best he could hope for. For the first time he thought with resentment of the dead, who would remain unchanged.

After the first few absences Marylee stopped calling the police; she knew it wouldn't do any good to ask his friends to look for him. It wasn't really necessary. Eventually somebody would telephone—he was passed out sick in the back of a waterfront bar, would she please come and take him home; he had gotten involved in a six-day poker game and gentle as he was when he was sober, he was raging now; if she didn't come get him, he was going to hurt himself or somebody else; he was in the hospital, he'd stepped in front of a slow-moving car. The last time he was gone for three weeks. He came to himself in the hospital, God knew what had happened in the time which had dropped out of his memory; there had been a fight, something worse had happened, he'd been hurt and he seemed to recall being stuck to the pavement, sleeping in a freezing rain. Marylee was by the bed, looking older than he could have imagined, and he could read his own death in her face. They didn't know yet that he had come back so the doctor continued to talk to Marylee: Heart failure, among other things. His lungs are filled with fluid, it's so far along I don't know how much we can do for him. Larkin knew that he couldn't get his breath; it was almost like drowning and he thought, God, how appropriate.

He did get better for a while as it turned out, and on a morning illumined by pallid winter sunlight he and Marylee began to talk. "I'm sorry for everything."

"Don't be."

"I have to make it up."

"You don't need to make anything up," she said. "This is my life, I'm satisfied."

"I should have stayed down there. It would have been better for everybody."

"Alvah, you didn't have to do anything. All you had to do was talk to me."

"I couldn't."

"I know."

"I couldn't. . . ." He was groping, trying to explain. "I just couldn't go on."

He understood then that what he had foreseen in the belly of the *Squalus* was not his own death or the guilt he expected to bear for the death of the others, but rather the prospect of having to continue, of having to face the unending, relentless possibilities for change. What he had resisted was not the death of the other men or even the death of Janny, whose young, perfect face he could see to this day, but the fact that he would have to continue and so descend, or decline, so that he may never have felt any guilt for the others but only resentment because they were fixed as they were, bright and young. They would never have to suffer, or age. He could feel his lungs filling again; he knew he was drowning at last. They would bring oxygen but it wouldn't help; he waited with satisfaction.

Larkin was weary, ready to go, but he had to complete the formula. "I made us all suffer."

She said with unexpected bitterness, "Somebody has to."

And so, waiting for oxygen, he understood that it must be the function of all the living to redeem the dead. He could see Janny's face but he said, with some urgency, "I have to get better."

Marylee said, "If only you'd talked to me."

Journey to the Center of the Earth

Jerome is in Nebraska to visit his father.

His dad lives in a model community located in the middle distance, at the point in the road where you think the line of shadows you see ahead is just about to congeal. At this juncture on this particular highway, you think the murky violet ridge along the horizon may be your first sight of the Rocky Mountains, but you can't be absolutely sure. Stay here and you'll never know; drive ten miles and the outline becomes clear.

This is where you make the turnoff for Bluemont. Take a sharp right on the two-track road through the foothills and in forty miles you're there. According to the literature his father's sent Jerome over the years since he left them, it's going to be some kind of Jerusalem—*We are the future of the world;* to Jerome it sounds crazy, exciting? His dad would never admit this, is firm in his use of the words *model community.*

It isn't much of a model.

The snapshots show a ring of outsized mobile homes beached on cinder block foundations, an assembly hall that promises more than it seems to deliver and a nineteenth-century house restored and painted like a wedding cake, and as for the rest? Half-finished foundations and a couple of huge, raw places in the earth, as if from excavations hastily filled and incompletely healed. Is this all? Jerome's dad says that when it's finished they will all live in contemporary houses with jutting redwood decks and crashing expanses of glass, but this will have to wait. Except for the self-styled mayor and leader of the group, the colonists are all stashed in those trailers, waiting for the town to rise. Their money always seems to be going into something else, but on the phone Jerome's father is vague about what. If it isn't the real thing, he thinks, then what's the point?

It's a strange place for Jerome, but here he is.

He has brought this on himself. Mostly he lives a normal life but when he goes home to visit he runs out of things to say. Caught short at Christmas, fresh out of words, he accidentally showed the brochure to his mom: mistake; the clouds around her head turned brown and started to boil.

"Lord," she said, squinting at the pictures as if she expected to find Jerome's dad walking around in them, this high, "what do you think is going on?"

Who was Jerome to tell her they were getting ready for the end of the world? He should have known she would figure it out: the prose, the strange device on the Bluemont sign.

"My God, he's in a religious sect."

"It's his life."

"He's your father," she said. So his mom has sent him to see about it. Although his folks have been divorced since he was ten, Jerome's mom can't stop worrying.

"I can't help it," she said. "It's never over with a person, no matter what you tell yourself."

"What do you want me to do?"

"I just want you to go."

What is he supposed to do, talk his dad out of this thing he's joined and bring him back to life as they know it? He doesn't think so. Is he supposed to be his mom's advance man, preparing the way? Certainly not. She is with Barry now. They are getting married in the spring.

So, what?

"A sect," she said, dispatching him. "I just . . ." She was at a loss. "I just want you to see if he's all right."

Maybe, Jerome thinks, she wants to find out if he's being held against his will.

He doesn't think so. The place isn't jail. It doesn't have to be; Jerome reasons, perhaps because he was brought up Catholic, that all religion is a captivity, souls held tight against their will.

So, hey. It may be what they want. And hey, what if they turn out to be right? A strange, almost sexual undercurrent draws him to this outside possibility. So he is here for his own reasons. Probably he spends too much time trying to make sense of things.

The last thing he did before he got here was check with her. Stopping at a diner outside Ogallalla, he'd called his mother collect. "What if these people are right?"

"God is God, but this is crazy," his mother said.

Still. But before he could raise this or demand marching orders she broke his heart with the good mom's farewell formula. Good old mom, dismissing him: "Be good. Have fun."

Jerome wants to see his father, is afraid. It's been so long; what are they to each other now? Although they have talked, phone calls from pads on the other side of town and in Maine and Morocco and San Francisco, he hasn't seen his dad since the divorce. After years of bopping around, his father has finally landed in one place. After a lot of confusion, his dad seems to be focused on one thing. Jerome is going to feel better about things if it turns out to be the right one.

Will his father be glad to see Jerome?

At least he'll be surprised.

Jerome is less anxious than depressed, driving in. Bluemont does not look good even in brochures; in person, in mud season, it's worse. In the waning spring light it looks not so much deserted as abandoned, the kind of place a reasonable God would turn his back on as too shabby to figure in any divine scheme. The tinny-looking pastel trailers are listing on their foundations, the assembly hall windows are boarded up against the winter cold and the wedding-cake house looks bedraggled and smirched. If these people are really onto something, there are no outward signs. Unless hardship is the whole thing.

My kingdom is not of this world, Jerome thinks. Yeah, right.

Negotiating the guck, he's grateful for the use of Barry's well-kept Jeep Cherokee, which has four-wheel drive. At least he'll be able to pull out of the mud when it's time to leave. Getting out of the car, he's also glad nobody's around. He really doesn't want to have to talk to anybody until he's seen his dad. It seems important to meet this place on his father's terms. He would like to wander around until he runs into his father, like, accidentally? Oh, hi.

When he gets out of the car, he's surprised by a watery feeling in his shins. It turns out Jerome is scared to death of meeting the other colonists, or whatever, is afraid of what he'll see rattling around behind the eyes. Flickering beyond this encounter with his father is the outside possibility of an absolute; the truth of this place, or his dad's life in this place, is strictly between the two of them. Somebody is coming out of the assembly hall—a woman in a big plaid jacket, quilted pants; she has her wool hat pulled way down, so, good. Jerome slouches along the board sidewalk with his chin buried in his shoulder, trying to look as though he comes here every day. He is so preoccupied by the mud squelching between the boards and over the rubber toes of his Nikes that when they pass, he doesn't even know whether the woman speaks. Automatically polite, he says hi and hurries on.

Finding his father turns out to be no problem. He is out behind his trailer splitting wood; at the right time Jerome just looks up and he's there.

"Dad!" The wind, emotion, something takes his voice away. His big moment and he can't make enough noise for his father to hear.

He looks the same, even from behind. In spite of the weather Justin is working with his coat off and his head uncovered; his fine hair is blowing, and where the drooping neck of the sweat-shirt exposes it, the skin on the back of his neck is fair. Jerome is unsettled by the change. When he was little his father was too big for him to see whole; now they are the same size.

Then. It is humiliating. Argh. Ghah. Jerome hears himself gabbling. "Hi. Bet you don't know who I am."

His father turns. "Oh, Jerome," he says, as if it's only been ten minutes. His face goes through a number of changes as he considers possible reasons for this visit. Stabbing Jerome in the heart, he lights on the wrong one. "What's the matter, are you in trouble?"

"No Dad, everything is fine."

"Oh son. Don't look like that." His father drops the axe and advances, thumping him into a hug.

Jerome is surprised by the force with which they collide. "Oh, hey."

Probably his father wishes he'd said the right thing to him.

Justin grins his same grin. "Come on in."

Inside is reassuring; the trailer is like a captain's cabin, everything trig; his dad's things look the same: books marching across the desk top, clipper ship bookends Justin took with him from the old house, baby picture of Jerome. He has added a laptop computer and a decanter set. Jerome touches one of the crystal stoppers.

"Your mom never forgave me for liberating the Waterford."

His mom never forgave him period.

In the old days his father used to be much heavier and wear a suit. Now he is skinny, mellow, aggressively laid back in the worn, silvery jeans and the stretched sweatshirt. He commands this space like the captain of a submarine. He is watching Jerome.

"Well, what do you think?"

"Nice," Jerome says, "but isn't it kind of small?"

"We're getting used to functioning in tight quarters." Without explaining, his father pulls out two lead crystal glasses Jerome remembers from his childhood. "Port?"

It's like the class reunion of a very small school. They are having alcohol because it's a party; because his dad still thinks of Jerome as ten years old, they are also having candy. The ashtray between them is filling up with little tags and silver foil.

In a strange way this seems perfectly right to Jerome—lounging on the neat convertible sofas with his dad in the late afternoon, eating Hershey's kisses and getting a buzz on. He focuses on the laptop computer, thinks it's a good sign. In case it turns out these people are crazy, his dad's probably here writing a book about them. Unless something better comes up, it's what he's going to tell his mom. But he stops his mouth with melting chocolate and doesn't ask. For a long time all they talk about are things they both remember from ten years ago, the house in Montclair, the dog they had, Jerome's troubles learning to ride his first two-wheeler, but the whole time Jerome is sitting with his eyes cracked too wide and his mouth open, listening for something he may not recognize.

He wants to come right out and ask his father, Where were you when you left us? He doesn't mean, Where did you go? He means, Where were you in your head? But hard as he tries to phrase the question, he has to get semi-blitzed before he can ask Justin anything, and when he does, all he can come up with is, "What happened to your house?"

His dad turns bland eyes to him. "What house?"

"I thought you guys were building modern houses."

"In time," his dad says. "Right now, there are more important things."

Jerome is just drunk enough to say, "The end of the world?"

Justin does not answer. "Supplies, for one."

Then while he slouches in the cushions with his mouth full, letting the chocolate melt and run around in there, his dad lays it out for him: how many of them there are in this community, what the arrangement is. They are pooling funds. The houses are not as important as laying in supplies. Like a materiel officer he numbers the things they have shored up against destruction, whether of society or the earth he does not say. At no point does his dad say anything crazy. The plan as he describes it is not religious, but pragmatic. He names some of the things they have: generators, food and water for sixty for a year, medical supplies, weapons, radiation detectors, a shopping list for Armageddon, but: what makes these people so sure it's coming? Jerome is afraid his dad will say God came down and told him.

But he doesn't. He just goes on about hydroponics and subsistence farming and the division of chores.

As his father talks, Jerome scours his speech for clues: as to why he's really here, what he thinks Jerome is doing here, because as he gets drunker and drunker, the tension builds until Jerome is squirming with urgency. He has to know what this man believes in. What's going to be expected of him.

"So that's the whole thing," his dad says finally, although it isn't.

When Jerome speaks, spit and chocolate overflow even though he's been careful to swallow beforehand. "I thought you were into something else."

His father does not ask the question.

Jerome can't frame the answer. "You know."

"I'll show you." Shoving a flashlight into his belt, the dad puts on his heavy jacket and throws a down vest at Jerome. "Here. You'll need an extra coat."

They go outside into the weak spring twilight, picking their way between lighted trailers like steaming jack-o'-lanterns that smell of a dozen dinners cooking. The few people caught outside at this hour are heading for their trailers with their heads down. They don't stop and they don't speak, but when father and son pass the wedding-cake house on their way to the periphery, a man comes out on the porch in his shirtsleeves to hail them; is this the leader?

"Justin," he says to Jerome's father.

"Jacquin."

Jerome wants to dig in his heels and take a good look at this person, but his father has him by the elbow now; all he has time to do is note the absence of beard or dreadlocks, whatever are the hallmarks. This is an ordinary-looking guy with a bland face trying to get a squint at Jerome.

When they don't stop, Jacquin calls, "New believer?"

"My son," Justin says, hurrying Jerome past.

Jacquin raises his hand in what looks like a blessing. Relieved, Jerome thinks, Oh, OK, so it is a religious thing. "Believer," he says. It's the word he's been waiting for but the speaker is in no respect his father, so . . . what?

His father says only, "Jacquin is in charge."

"Readiness," the man on the porch says after them.

"Readiness." Jerome whips his head around. "Is that the whole thing?"

The question is imprecise; Jerome's dad doesn't bother to answer. He runs ahead like a big kid calling Come play. "Come over here. Come on down and you'll see."

When Jerome catches up Justin is standing in the middle of one of the raw places, in the mixture of mud and rubble that covers a recent excavation. A cement mixer leans next to a makeshift railing around an open place. He turns on his flashlight and shines it into the hole. The sides are shored up by cement forms, suggesting that whatever work is going on here is only partly done. From the top Jerome can't see how deep the ladder goes, but his father has already turned on his flashlight and started down.

At the bottom his dad lands on a metal surface with a leaden *klunk*. Planting his feet on either side of a wheel, he begins opening a hatch. Inside, another ladder descends into blackness. Then his dad finds the switch and the place lights up.

"What's this?"

"Shelter," Justin says. "It's not finished yet."

"What for?"

"Protection."

What? "You're *all* coming down here?"

"Half of us. We're fitting out two."

Following him down, Jerome is dizzy with the complications. His mind keeps zigzagging between the two shelters: Will they be able to talk? How will they know if each other are all right? If somebody's left behind? Whether everybody fits? Who's gone to which? Here two minutes and he's already feeling claustrophobic; it's like being inside a cigar case, this funny metal cylinder that smells. How are they going to stand it for a year?

"Took us a long time to work out the best thing to do the job," his father says. "We've buried propane tanks."

"In case of what?"

"Whatever happens," his father says.

He lets Jerome take it in: the double row of bunks at the far end of the enclosure, lights strung like Christmas bulbs, from exposed wires, wooden flooring that must hide the year's worth of rations his father has told him about. The floor orients him. Without it they would be like astronauts in free-fall. Jerome is giddy, short of breath; his dad has brought him all this way and showed him all this and told him everything and at no time and in no way has he mentioned the name of God. It would have been so neat, something to hang onto, that Jerome could pin it all on: the persistence or the folly of faith. But his father is done explaining.

When Jerome can't think of anything to say his father says, "We stay down here until it's safe." He runs out of steam, suddenly, and sits down on the wooden flooring with his back hunched to accommodate the curve in the metal wall. The tank seems hollow, leaden and echoing, cold. Jerome sits down next to him. They probably look like refugees hiding from World War II in the British underground.

Cold and silent, Jerome is crowded by misgivings. Maybe he has attached too much to this. He imagined his father would get him down here and explain at least; tell him some truth. Either that or demonstrate that he's completely crazy, leaving Jerome free to hug him goodbye and walk away.

Instead he just sits here next to Jerome in the dank shelter without saying anything.

It is almost unbearable, the tension between the two of them wedged here in the curve of the cylinder, and yet there is no reason for it that Jerome can see. They're just hanging, adrift in a welter of particles. There's too much going on and none of it resolved; his father has hurt everybody and run away from everything and replaced it with this.

Sitting shoulder to shoulder with his dad Jerome thinks maybe he's come all this way to let it all out and get it over with; raging, he could just let his father have it: How could you do this to us? How could you run away and bust up our family?

"Don't be too hard on your father," his mom said at the time. "He can't help it." Probably he can't, Jerome thinks, and even if he can, there is no way for Jerome to charge him with it now. What would be the point? It's something they can't change, that happened years ago. But this whole thing, this awful *place*. Sitting here under tons of earth, Jerome needs, what: to explain or justify whatever his father thinks he's doing here. If he has come here and is doing this because of either sex or religion it may make some kind of sense, but there is no sign of a girlfriend anywhere in the trailer and this is only a bomb shelter.

Jerome would just like to be able to go back home with some real reason that he can lay out for everyone, so he can call it finished. He wants something he can point to and say, OK. There.

His father surprises him. "I suppose you're here to see if I'm crazy."

Caught in the act, Jerome starts; his head bonks the metal wall. "You really think the end of the world is coming?"

The gaze his father turns on him is empty, without guile. "Does it really matter?"

"I think so," Jerome says.

"And if it's true?"

This is a trick question; if Jerome believes it, the true course of logic followed to its absolute limit dictates the shelter, everything. He has to beg the question. "But dad, we've stopped being scared of the Russians. Getting nuked. The war."

The look his father turns on him is careful, lucid. "That's only one of the names for it."

"Ah." Jerome squirms. The air in here is becoming intolerable; he pushes. "Names for what?" Armageddon? He is intent, squinting as if he can see the answer written in air inside his father's open mouth.

"Whatever."

Jerome is stifling. "For God's *sake*."

Then his father gets as close as he is going to come. "There are worse things than living at the edge of last things."

Jerome says angrily, "That's it?"

"What did you think you were going to get from me?"

Better than this; too much; he doesn't know.

"Whatever it is, whatever threatens us . . ." The look his father turns on him is careful, lucid. "You might as well boil it all down to something you can prepare for. Can do something about. And start doing it." And then his father, who is supposed to be the adult here, gives him a noogie on the shoulder, grinding the knuckles in with a grin. "But, hey. It doesn't matter if I believe in it. I like it here."

"That's all?"

"It's as good as any of the reasons people give for the things they do."

The logic! "God, Dad." Jerome jumps to his feet; the clammy air is killing him; he can hardly stand it. "Are you ever going to let us out of here?"

"I guess I'd better cancel your reservation," Justin says lightly.

At least there is some logic; Jerome lets his breath out all at once. "Damn straight."

His father pushes him up the ladder. "You first. I'm starved."

The stars are out when they reach the top and explode into the evening air. Jerome's dizzy all over again, this time with relief, delight at being released; Justin catches some of his son's joy. "Come on," he says, "we're out of here. The last of the big spenders is going to take you into Ogallala and buy you a steak."

Then at the end, when Jerome has almost forgotten about it, he gets, if not exactly what he thought he came for, this; it's as good as he's going to get.

They are standing in the Bluemont parking area in the pink early morning, getting ready to say goodbye. His dad, with his face full of incomplete good intentions is looking at Jerome, who's waiting next to Barry's Jeep Cherokee, kicking the cleated tire. They've already hugged and Jerome is about to get in the car and go but he can't just leave it like this; he is sick of being cool.

"God, Dad," he cries—he wants to get it all back: himself, when little, the family he used to have. Belief. "I didn't come all this way for this."

"What do you want?"

He is astounded to hear himself: "I love you. I want you to come with me!"

"Too late." His father shrugs. "You know. But you can come back here any time you want."

His voice sinks so deep only he can hear it. "Oh God. Oh Dad."

So he has to get into the car. He's already shut the door on himself and rolled down the window to catch any last words when his father blunders into it; his smile is beautiful.

"Be good," Justin says, inadvertently recalling the old pattern, this: that their lives together are all of a piece. "Have fun."

Winter

It was late fall when he come to us, there was a scum of ice on all the puddles and I could feel the winter cold and fearsome in my bones, the hunger inside me was already uncurling, it would pace through the first of the year but by spring it would be raging like a tiger, consuming me until the thaw when Maude could hunt again and we would get the truck down the road to town. I was done canning but I got the tomatoes we had hanging in the cellar and I canned some more; Maude went out and brought back every piece of meat she could shoot and all the grain and flour and powdered milk she could bring in one truckload, we had to lay in everything we could before the snow came and sealed us in. The week he come Maude found a jackrabbit stone dead in the road, it was frozen with its feet sticking straight up, and all the meat hanging in the cold-room had froze. Friday there was rime on the grass and when I looked out I seen footprints in the rime, I said Maude, someone is in the playhouse and we went out and there he was. He was asleep in the mess of clothes we always dressed up in, he had his head on the velvet gown my mother wore to the Exposition and his feet on the satin gown she married Father in, he had pulled her feather boa around his neck and her fox fur was wrapped around his loins.

Before he come, Maude and me would pass the winter talking

about how it used to be, we would call up the past between us and look at it and Maude would end by blaming me. I could of married either Lister Hoffman or Harry Mead and left this place for good if it hadn't been for you, Lizzie. I'd tell her, Hell, I never needed you. You didn't marry them because you didn't marry them, you was scared of it and you would use me for an excuse. She would get mad then. It's a lie. Have it your way, I would tell her, just to keep the peace.

We both knew I would of married the first man that asked me, but nobody would, not even with all my money, nobody would ask me because of the taint. If nobody had of known then some man might of married me, but I went down to the field with Miles Harrison once while Father was still alive, and Miles and me, we almost, except that the blackness took me, right there in front of him, and so I never did. Nobody needed to know, but then Miles saw me fall down in the field. I guess it was him that put something between my teeth so I wouldn't bite my tongue, but when I come to myself he was gone. Next time I went to town they all looked at me funny, some of them would try and face up to me and be polite but they was all jumpy, thinking would I do it right there in front of them, would I froth much, would they get hurt, as soon as was decent they would say Excuse me, I got to, anything to get out of there fast. When I run into Miles after that day he wouldn't look at me and there hasn't been a man near me since then, not in more than fifty years, but Miles and me, we almost, and I have never stopped thinking about that.

Now Father is gone and my mother is gone and even Lister Hoffman and Miles Harrison and half the town kids that used to laugh at me, they are all gone, but Maude still reproaches me, we sit after supper and she says If it hadn't been for you I would have grandchildren now and I tell her I would of had them before ever she did because she never liked men, she would only suffer them to get children and that would be too much trouble, it would hurt. That's a lie, Lizzie, she would say, Harry and me used to . . . and I would tell her You never, but Miles and me . . . . Then we would both think about being young and having people's hands on us but memory turns Maude bitter and she can never leave it at that, she says, It's all your fault, but I know in my heart that people make their lives what they want them, and all she ever wanted was to be locked in here with nobody to make demands on her, she wanted to stay in this house with me, her dried-up sister, cold and safe, and if the hunger is on her, it has come on her late.

After a while we would start to make up stuff: Once I went with a boy all the way to Portland. . . . Once I danced all night and half the morning, he wanted to kiss me on the place where my elbow bends. . . . We would try to spin out the winter, but even that was not enough and so we would always be left with the hunger; no matter how much we laid in, the meat was always gone before the thaw and I suppose it was really our lives we was judging but we would decide nothing in the cans looked good to us and so we would sit and dream and hunger and wonder if we would die of it, but finally the thaw would come and Maude would look at me and sigh: If only we had another chance.

Well now perhaps we will.

We found him in the playhouse, maybe it was seeing him being in the playhouse, where we pretended so many times, asleep in the middle of my mother's clothes or maybe it was something of mine; there was this boy, or man, something about him called up our best memories, there was promise wrote all over him. I am too old, I am all dried out, but I have never stopped thinking about that one time, and seeing that boy there, I could pretend he was Miles and I was still young. I guess he sensed us, he woke up fast and went into a crouch, maybe he had a knife, and then I guess he saw it was just too big old ladies in Army boots, he said, I run away from the Marines, I need a place to sleep.

Maude said, I don't care what you need, you got to get out of here, but when he stood up he wobbled. His hair fell across his head like the hair on a boy I used to know and I said, Maude, why don't you say yes to something just this once.

He had on this denim shirt and pants like no uniform I ever

seen and he was saying, Two things happened, I found out I might have to shoot somebody in the war and then I made a mistake and they beat me so I cut out of there. He smiled and he looked open. I stared hard at Maude and Maude finally looked at me and said, All right, come up to the house and get something to eat.

He said his name was Arnold but when we asked him Arnold what, he said Never mind. He was in the kitchen by then, he had his head bent over a bowl of oatmeal and some biscuits I had made, and when I looked at Maude she was watching the way the light slid across his hair. When we told him our names he said, You are both beautiful ladies, and I could see Maude's hands go up to her face and she went into her room and when she came back I saw she had put color on her cheeks. While we was alone he said how good the biscuits was and wasn't that beautiful silver, did I keep it polished all by myself and I said well yes, Maude brings in supplies but I am in charge of the house and making all the food. She come back then and saw us with our heads together and said to Arnold, I guess you'll be leaving soon.

I don't know, he said, they'll be out looking for me with guns and dogs.

That's no never mind of ours.

I never done anything bad in the Marines, we just had different ideas. We both figured it was something worse but he looked so sad and tired and besides, it was nice to have him to talk to, he said, I just need a place to hole up for a while.

Maude said, You could always go back to your family.

He said, They never wanted me. They was always mean hearted, not like you.

I took her aside and said, It wouldn't kill you to let him stay on. Maude, it's time we had a little life around here.

There won't be enough food for three.

He won't stay long. Besides, he can help you with the chores.

She was looking at his bright hair again, she said, like it was all my doing, If you want to let him stay I guess we can let him stay.

He was saying, I could work for my keep.

All right, I said, you can stay on until you get your strength.

My heart jumped. A man, I thought. A man. How can I explain it? It was like being young, having him around. I looked at Maude and saw some of the same things in her eyes, hunger and hope, and I thought, You are ours now, Arnold, you are all ours. We will feed you and take care of you and when you want to wander we will let you wander, but we will never let you go.

Just until things die down a little, he was saying.

Maude had a funny grin. Just until things die down.

Well it must of started snowing right after dark that afternoon, because when we all waked up the house was surrounded. I said, Good thing you got the meat in, Maude, and she looked out, it was still blowing snow and it showed no signs of stopping; she looked out and said, I guess it is.

He was still asleep, he slept the day through except he stumbled down at dusk and dreamed over a bowl of my rabbit stew, I turned to the sink and when I looked back the stew was gone and the biscuits was gone and all the extra in the pot was gone, I had a little flash of fright, it was all disappearing too fast. Then Maude come over to me and hissed, The food, he's eating all the food and I looked at his brown hands and his tender neck and I said, It don't matter, Maude, he's young and strong and if we run short he can go out into the snow and hunt. When we looked around next time he was gone, he had dreamed his way through half a pie and gone right back to bed.

Next morning he was up before the light, we sat together around the kitchen table and I thought how nice it was to have a man in the house, I could look at him and imagine anything I wanted. Then he got up and said, Look, I want to thank you for everything, I got to get along now, and I said, You can't, and he said, I got things to do, I been here long enough, but I told him You can't, and took him over to the window. The sun was up by then and there it was, snow almost to the window ledges, like we have every winter, and all the trees was shrouded, we could watch the sun take the snow and make it sparkle and I said, Beautiful snow, beautiful, and he only shrugged and said, I guess I'll have to wait till it clears off some. I touched his shoulder. I guess you will. I knew not to tell him it would never clear off, not until late spring; maybe he guessed, anyway he looked so sad I gave him Father's silver snuffbox to cheer him up.

He would divide his time between Maude and me, he played Rook with her and made her laugh so hard she gave him her pearl earrings and the brooch Father brought her back from Quebec. I gave him Grandfather's diamond stickpin because he admired it, and for Christmas we gave him the cameos and Father's gold-headed cane. Maude got the flu over New Year's and Arnold and me spent New Year's Eve together, I mulled some wine and he hung up some of Mama's jewelry from the center light, and touched it and made it twirl. We lit candles and played the radio, New Year's Eve in Times Square and somebody's Make-Believe Ballroom, I went to pour another cup of wine and his hand was on mine on the bottle, I knew my lips was red for once and next day I gave him Papa's fur-lined coat.

I guess Maude suspected there was something between us, she looked pinched and mean when I went in with her broth at lunch, she said, Where were you at breakfast and I said, Maude, it's New Year's day, I thought I would like to sleep in for once. You were with him. I thought, If she wants to think that about me, let her, and I let my eyes go sleepy and I said, We had to see the New Year in, didn't we? She was out of bed in two days, I have never seen anybody get up so fast after the flu. I think she couldn't stand us being where she couldn't see what we was up to every living minute.

Then I got sick and I knew what torture it must have been for her just laying there, I would call Maude and I would call her, and sometimes she would come and sometimes she wouldn't come and when she finally did look in on me I would say, Maude, where have you been, and she would only giggle and not answer. There was meat cooking all the time, roasts and chops and chicken fricassee, when I said Maude, you're going to use it up, she would only smile and say, I just had to show him who's who in the kitchen, he tells me I'm a better cook than you ever was. After a while I got up, I had to even if I was dizzy and like to throw up, I had to get downstairs where I could keep an eye on them. As soon as I was up to it I made a roast of venison that would put hair on an egg and after that we would vie with each other in the kitchen, Maude and me. Once I had my hand on the skillet handle and she come over and tried to take it away, she was saying, Let me serve it up for him, I said, You're a fool, Maude, I cooked this, and she hissed at me, through the steam, It won't do you no good, Lizzie, it's me he loves, and I just pushed her away and said, You goddam fool, he loves me, and I give him my amethysts just to prove it. A couple of days later I couldn't find neither of them nowhere, I thought I heard noises up in the back room and I went up and if they was in there they wouldn't answer, the door was locked and they wouldn't say nothing, not even when I knocked and knocked and knocked. So the next day I took him up in my room and we locked the door and I told him a story about every piece in my jewel box, even the chap ones, when Maude tapped and whined outside the door we would just shush, and when we did come out and she said, All right, Lizzie, what was you doing in there, I only giggled and wouldn't tell.

She shouldn't of done it, we was all sitting around the table after dinner and she looked at me hard and said, You know something, Arnold, I wouldn't get too close to Lizzie, she has fits. Arnold only tried to look like it didn't matter, but after Maude went to bed I went down to make sure it was all right. He was still in the kitchen, whittling, and when I tried to touch his hand he pulled away.

I said, Don't be scared, I only throw one in a blue moon.

He said, That don't matter.

Then what's the matter?

I don't know, Miss Lizzie, I just don't think you trust me.

Course I trust you, Arnold, don't I give you everything?

He just looked sad. Everything but trust.

I owe you so much, Arnold, you make me feel so young.

He just smiled for me then. You look younger, Miss Lizzie, you been getting younger every day I been here.

You did it.

If you let me, I could make you really young.

Yes, Arnold, yes.

But I have to know you trust me.

Yes, Arnold.

So I showed him where the money was. By then it was past midnight and we was both tired, he said, Tomorrow, and I let him go off to get his rest.

I don't know what roused us both and brought us out into the hall but I bumped into Maude at dawn, we was both standing in our nightgowns like two ghosts. We crept downstairs together and there was light in the kitchen, the place where we kept the money was open, empty, and there was a crack of light in the door to the coldroom. I remember looking through and thinking, The meat is almost gone. Then we opened the door a crack wider and there he was, he had made a sledge, he must of sneaked down there and worked on it every night. It was piled with stuff, and now he had the door to the outside open, he had dug himself a ramp out of the snow and he was lashing some home-made snowshoes on his feet, in another minute he would of cut out of there.

When he heard us he turned.

I had the shotgun and Maude had the axe.

We said, We don't care about the stuff, Arnold. How could we tell him it was our youth he was taking away?

He looked at us, walleyed. You can have it all, just let me out.

He was going to get away in another minute, so Maude let him have it with the axe.

Afterwards we closed the way to the outside and stood there and looked at each other, I couldn't say what was in my heart so I only looked at Maude, we was both sad, sad, I said, The food is almost gone.

Maude said, Everything is gone. We'll never make it to spring.

I said, We have to make it to spring.

Maude looked at him laying there. You know what he told me? He said, I can make you young.

Me too, I said. There was something in his eyes that made me believe it.

Maude's eyes was glittering, she said, The food is almost gone.

I knew what she meant, he was going to make us young. I don't know how it will work in us, but he is going to make us young, it will be as if the fits had never took me, never in all them years. Maude was looking at me, waiting, and after a minute I looked square at her and I said, I know.

So we et him.

The Jonahs

My name is Bartlett J. Daniels and my father is the director of public works in Cobleskill, New York. I myself am a librarian. The name of the whale that has swallowed me is . . ." The others waited with gleaming, upturned faces and eyes that gave back the fluorescent ceiling lights, but even now, standing before them in the basement activity room, he could not say Ticia's name and made a hasty substitution, finishing, not altogether incorrectly, ". . . envy."

The minister's mouth, which he had stretched wide in the effort to concentrate, clicked shut: validation. Yes. This is one of the problems good men bring to us. Some of the Jonahs nodded; others lowered their eyes and shrugged with little sighs of fatigue because whatever its name the monster is large and swallows many. Still their smiles, the sleek, combed heads and earnest Christian faces argued that if they had found peace so could anyone. They sat with shoulders raised slightly, not so much supporting as wearing the body of the church that rose above the basement meeting room—the high spine with bowed gothic arches; they could have been inside a giant rib cage, or in the superstructure of a sailing ship with its curved struts. They were not exactly conscious of this; they were, rather, *accustomed*; for the moment he too felt this comfort of enclosure: Bartlett J. Daniels safe among his brethren, borne along on the great voyage whose destination was hard to reach and even harder to divine.

Is it fair to them to name one enemy when I am really facing another?
When he thought of Ticia his body melted. In a life which had never quite lived up to his hopes for it, she signified the possibility that this might change.

Ticia's long hair was carelessly gathered in an intricate wooden loop. He wanted to catch loose strands in his mouth, leave the marks of his teeth on her neck. Together they would do—what? Whatever they wanted. Everything. His wife Ellen kept her hair short; she liked things neat. When he watched her comb it, his wife's indifference made him quake with guilt.

Imagining Ticia's body, he lost track; anticipation devoured him.

"We all know envy." The minister placed this like a bookmark, reminding Bartlett where he had left off. In the lexicon of guilt and restitution, he knew all the words. Fluorescent bars glinted in his glasses as he smiled.

Certain of the Jonahs leaned forward slightly, coaching, drawing Bartlett along: Are you like us? Yes, you are like us! Each man carried something. Each secretly believed his pain was the greatest, his story the most profound.

What faith, Bartlett thought, to be so sure of the significance of their own struggles. What generosity—asking him to join: men's group of the faithful, questing, troubled; easy allusion to wrestling with the Almighty, only the best men can, you have that look. . . . Lord, he thought, does it show? Did Ellen put them onto me?

"Nothing you can say will surprise us."

What vanity.

He tried to explain. "When the wife and I visit at my brother's house I am aware that it has always just been painted. They have plushy carpets that you can sink into, and matching chairs and sofas. My brother has two cars. Unlike Dad and me, Ernest eschewed the life of public service. He works for a major corporation."

It was not envy he felt, walking into his brother's house. Ernie's house was very nice but not what he wanted. The silk upholstery was an unpleasant color, the flocked wallpaper too flossy, the decor too heavy-handed to be in good taste. Using an intercom to monitor the front door was preposterous. ("It's me," he had cried the first time, standing in the snow. "Let me in Ernie, you know goddam well it's your brother.") Still, Ernie's house, like Ernie, gave off the sheen of prosperity.

What troubled him then was the sharp nip of regret because his own seemed run-down by comparison—the veneer on his furniture peeling in the gas heat, sagging plaster so loose that his wallpaper drooped in several places. There were stains in his hardwood floors and mildew in the bathroom yet it was not even this that bothered him; it was, rather, creeping discomfort, the unnerving sense of living a mistake he had not yet identified. When he and Ellen came home from those visits to Ernie's it was always raining. She was edgy, his children untidy and querulous. He had trouble getting up in the mornings. He knew even before he got out of bed what it would be like: walking through a house he could not afford to repair, moving from one threadbare carpet to another.

When they came home from one Christmas at his brother's he spent too much on an oriental for the living room, yes it would sit uneasily with their things, which perhaps he intended—*We'll have to throw out everything and start over.*

"Good God. Where did that come from?" Ellen said the one worst thing. "You know we can't afford it."

Did she always have to have dark circles around her eyes? "Don't think about that. Take it for what it is. It's a present."

"Lord, Bartlett, you gave me plenty of presents when we were at Ernie's." She sounded like a polite little girl. "I love my new blender."

"I guess I'm not very good at presents." He remembered how Ellen had looked, sitting with the blender on her lap. Adorning his captive princess, his brother always gave semiprecious stones or tribal-looking chains. This was, Bartlett thought, a matter of how you regarded a person. (Talking one midnight, murmuring over the miles, Ticia told him: *Ernie only sees my body.* Not me, Bartlett thought. Not me.)

"They were lovely." Ellen, that tone! "It's fine."

"Still." Proffering the rug like an expensive pelt, he recognized her expression. "You don't like it."

"I'm sorry. It's the cost," she said and then in one of her extraordinary moments of prescience she added, "It's going to ruin us. What on earth did you think you were doing?"

"Nothing," he said, "I wasn't doing anything."

"So," said the oldest of the Jonahs, a regretful banker whose children had turned out badly, "the name of the monster that devours you is *things.*"

"No," Bartlett said with complete certainty. "This is not about things."

Even in the harsh light of the meeting room Ticia's voice curled about him like the night, insubstantial, seductive. When they were together—bodies, breath mingled, he would have everything. *Oh Lord*, he thought, *is there a name for my indiscretion?*

"Perhaps," he continued, choking on guilt, "I have done nothing to be ashamed of."

How could he be sure of this, when he was consumed by desire for Ticia, whom he never saw? How could he explain to them?

Taking the Jonahs through Ernie's expensive home, describing the appointments, Bartlett thought it had been his misfortune to make bad choices. Returning the oriental rug they could not afford, he had been forced back on his own insufficiency.

Once, accidentally, Ellen found him sitting with his head in his hands. She knelt next to him. It was hard for him to understand how even when they made love her arms seemed so stiff and her breasts so unyielding. When they were first married this had surprised him. Now everything did.

Spare, dry, anxious, she tried to console him. "Bartlett, what's the matter?"

God! There it was!

This—everything—rose in his mouth but there was no way to

tell her. Instead he heard himself raging, "Why is it that everything in our house is broken?"

She did her best. That month Ellen made new draperies for the living room—an off-white, against the day when they might be able to afford the Persian rug.

He told the Jonahs, "My brother heats his swimming pool. Once we went swimming outdoors in November." There was Ernie looking tanned in late autumn, well-muscled and prosperous, sitting on the terrace while the women bobbed in the pool, Ernie offering him a Glen plaid suit he said he never wore because it was too loud for Washington. The cold air blanched Ellen's lips and her narrow shoulders. There was Bartlett, not a Jonah but a Lazarus, saying no thank you it was not his color. On a little table by the pool there was a pitcher of lemonade. By the late afternoon light, Ernie's children played badminton with Bartlett's children. Badminton!

"My brother shows me his cars." This was too complicated to explain to this audience: Ernie opening sleek doors to thump pale leather upholstery. Take that! Cain and Abel eternally grappling. "Sometimes I hate him," Bartlett said, waiting for lightning to strike him.

The listening Jonahs did not judge, or censure; perhaps fixed on their own performances, each waiting for his turn, they only accepted. The minister, who had heard much worse, stretched and tilted his head attentively.

Studying their smooth faces, Bartlett saw no trace of what he had just told them. God they were kind. He began to suspect that, trying to make him feel at home, the Jonahs only pretended to misery. They might even make up equivalent sins to tell him, to make him feel less guilty. Enclosed and reinforced by what they did together here, safe in the arms of the church, they were in fact smooth as so many polished stones. Like Ernie, they wore the sheen of prosperity, the sleek skin of certainty. He saw himself as from above—a wild bird thrust into the dovecote, ragged and out of place.

The minister began. "Even the best of us knows envy."

There they were, then: *the best of us*. Secure in religion. The saved. How could he believe, when he didn't know? Where did he fit in?

The youngest of the Jonahs, who had gone to school with Bartlett, said, "There is not a man among us who hasn't felt some of the same things."

That's what you think.

How could he explain the terrible disparity—the four of them going out together, walking to the movies at Dupont Circle, Bartlett and Ellen, Ticia and Ernie moving like swimmers through the August heat. Ernie and Ticia always ran slightly ahead, perhaps so Bartlett would have to see his brother's hand passing lightly across his brother's wife's tight haunch as with perfunctory fondness he let his own hand smooth Ellen's crumpled linen, feeling her slack waist; after the movies there would be drinks at Ernie's house—Ernie's cognac, Ernie's Waterford snifters, Ernie's things.

How could they know what it was like, two families moiling in close quarters, the sexual tension? In Ernie's house he was almost overpowered by the bodies: his, Ellen's, theirs, going to and from the bathroom in the night, the men and women passed *this close;* how was he supposed to say in front of these grave men what most disturbed him: that his brother always looked freshly fucked?

It was going to be months before Bartlett could tell the truth. The form his love took was as hard to explain as it was to understand. In a lifetime of bad choices, he had not even chosen this. It had been given.

Bartlett's voice broke because he still could not tell them her name. "Ah—sh—his wife doesn't work. She doesn't have to. She spends her time on the marriage. And . . ." he said, leaving out the noun. Telling them about his love, he made it real, ". . . that is the name of the whale that has devoured me."

"God bless you."

The men rose and gathered around to shake his hand—together in the whale, although for each it had a different name. Bartlett smiled shakily and let them surround him: kindred because each carried his trouble like a jewel to be treasured.

Like the Jonahs, the minister had his own treasure—a collection of these painful admissions. He may have been thinking: *Welcome aboard.* He said, "Let us pray together."

At home that night Ellen looked at him carefully, but if she understood there was a difference in him, she could not put a name to it. Instead she put her arms around him and tried to move close, but her body was—still her body.

Alarmed, he said, "What's the matter?"

She sniffed his neck, put her face in his hair. "Bartlett, are you seeing somebody?"

"My God, I was at the church."

"Are you?"

"Dear God Ellen, no." It was the truth. It wasn't the truth.

What he did: it didn't matter. It did not. It really didn't. It made no detectable difference in the way he was with Ellen, or Ellen was with him. It was simply a matter of concentration— where he put his heart. All he had to show for his passion was certain thoughts. The lie, if it was a lie.

He told himself, as if explaining to the Jonahs, *Everybody has to have something to go on.*

He needed this, about Ticia. Lived for it. Too much of the time he was caught by circumstance, moving through days not of his own making, which he supposed was why this accident of love exercised so much power over him. Who wouldn't cherish such a passion? Who wouldn't retreat to a secret place inside to gloat?

He was sorry about Ellen. When they got married they had expected to be happy. His paychecks, which he had thought would take care of anything they might *need*, barely met expenses. Starting out, he had not conceived of the power of *wants*. It wasn't Ellen's fault nothing had come out the way they thought it would, or that they both had to work day and night just to keep going. Exhausted, she came to bed both suppliant and unyielding, a locked safe with the combination hidden in an inaccessible place. He wondered if she knew that when he tried to reach her center she barely moved; rigid with disapproval, she suffered him. When he cried out it was not in passion but lament. The good wife, Ellen would whisper anxiously, "All right?" which he knew better than to answer with a question; she always added, "Just as long as it's all right," and could not know how much this made him want to weep.

He could not for the life of him point to the moment when it changed from what he and Ellen had hoped for to what it was. How had it happened? Whose fault was it anyway?

At work, at least, things were all right. Like his father, Bartlett was a public servant, a calling which he believed in as firmly as he believed whatever it was that took him to the church for meetings of the Jonahs. It had not so much to do with God, he thought, as with belonging—being part of a society that worked in an orderly fashion. He despised Ernie for selling out, while he commanded a large branch of the Public Library. Its order was his order. It was with such pride that the master must contemplate his ship. He had a place here. Standing in the main reading room he could feel it. He was protected, surrounded, reinforced. Like the oak paneling and the leaded windows in the foyer with its striated green marble floor, he had substance.

Then, God, why did he begin with Ticia?

Some nights he stood in the upstairs hall of his ramshackle house with his eyes shut and his breath hot in the mouth of the telephone, whispering, "Oh my God I do love you, Ticia," to which she always answered surely but faintly, as though the words had to travel all those miles on foot: "I do too."

On other nights he fed on what they had said to each other last time, imagining what they would do when they finally joined.

They exchanged presents by mail: earrings she would be afraid to wear, a white silk aviator's scarf he kept at the office.

She sent short, loving notes to him in care of the library, perhaps because women know how observant women are of what comes into the house. Writing her at home, where she was alone all day and always intercepted the mail, he composed long, passionate letters, controlled, beautiful. At this distance he was eloquent.

How had they started? Did she give him a sign? He did not think so. He only knew when he and Ellen came home from that last August visit, he knew something was different. Passing in the hall in the night, Bartlett and Ticia had brushed. He had felt her hand on his. It was like being caught in a tremor that jars the earth in such a way that afterward things look the same, but everything has shifted. When had he called her first? One smoky night in autumn when the cold air was quick with promise and he was filled to splitting with anticipation. He had spun through the house, trying to swallow desire, yearning at windows; it seemed everything he wanted was outside in the dark, just about to come flying in. Tormented, he found himself in the upstairs hall, gripping the telephone. Ellen was asleep in the bedroom. What if she woke and overheard? He did not care. He had to talk to Ticia, and she—he was amazed when she answered the phone on the first ring and did not so much fall as plunge into the conversation; to his astonishment she had to talk to him.

Ticia, I had to talk to you.

Her breath was moist; he could hear it. *It's you. At last.*

At last! *You might as well know I love you.*

Astonishingly, her words rushed out to meet him. *And I do too!*

He was trembling. *What are we going to do about it?*

Once again she astounded him. *We are already doing it.*

I want us to be together.

Lover, we are.

Thus their phone calls, at length, on many nights, not so much changing his life as raising the possibility that it could change. For the moment, this was enough. He made so many calls that eventually he thought to charge them to the library number, not quite forestalling Ellen's dry comment: "All these calls to Washington! For sibling rivals, you and Ernie certainly have a lot to say."

Whenever he telephoned, Ticia's voice met his with passion; separated like that, yearning in the dark, they did not so much plan as imagine making love, the ways in which their bodies would come together. For whatever reasons, they did not try to meet.

Bartlett carried his secret like a talisman, something extraordinary he had been given. It was precisely because it was unrealized that this love was precious. It would never be tarnished or diminished by time or age or the gap that fell between the intention and the act. Mystically joined, he and Ticia were both something *more*—better than the content of their lives.

When he went out now it was with a difference. No matter what else happened, he had this. When he came in at night he could smile at Ellen and not falter; he could sit comfortably with the consequences of wrong choices because he had also chosen this; he was in love, and he was loved.

All day he did the right things, good man, stoutly living forward, pulled through hard days by those scattered whispered conversations, the magnet that drew his heart. No matter what went wrong he could reach into the night and touch Ticia, feeding on her, and when they had whispered and wept he could still slip back into bed in the peace of rectitude. He could lie there with Ticia's words curling about him like naked fingers and at the same time think: *I have done nothing wrong here. I keep certain things from her, but I am still faithful to my wife.*

If it were lust, he told himself, by now we would have met. No I am not in love with her body, he told himself, although it was all he thought about. I love her for what she *is*. But what is that? He did not know. He only knew that what they had was wonderful, and that he had to keep it the way it was.

Thus he struggled weekly before the Jonahs, not because he wanted to change, but because they kept telling him he was a Christian, and therefore it seemed important to try. So long as he did not name Ticia out loud, he would not have to give her up. He had not done anything. He enjoyed infidelity without the consequences, longed to enjoy it without guilt. The minister said, "We want you to learn to feel good about yourself." Very well. As long as they did not meet, Bartlett could sit among these good men because, like them, he was trying to be good. It was important to him to keep coming here. In the absence of God, he thought, he would make do with the church.

On one of those Wednesdays, he thought: *I don't hate our house. I haven't fallen out of love with Ellen, I only want things to be different.*

Meeting in early December, he understood why he could never name her in this company. Not here, in the basement of the church. Filled with his secret, warmed by it, he thought, with some clarity, *I don't even really love Ticia, at least not that way.* This frightened him. Wind gusted through his head. He looked around anxiously but nobody else in the room had felt it. Then the wind, or whatever it was, shuddered to a stop. *Then what am I doing? What did I think I was doing all this time?*

The light in the room changed slightly, as subtly as the sky in tornado season—a change meaning not that something dangerous was going to happen, but that it might. He was frightened. Slouching in the circle of metal folding chairs while one of the others talked about his battle with—was it alcohol?—Bartlett slid his chair back slightly so that he was more or less behind the sturdy realtor on his right. He was trying to hide, and could not.

Ticia could not protect him, nor his clandestine love, that he had put on like a cloak. A bolt of lightning, it smote him: *Oh my God I hate my life.*

He pushed his chair back and got up and tried to creep out without disturbing them. With his mouth scrolling in concern the minister tiptoed to the door to intercept him. "I can't stay," Bartlett whispered, passionately, "I can't stay!"

That night he stormed his wife, swooping down as if on an undefended fortress. "Oh Ellen, I've sold some bonds. We'll borrow on the life insurance, we have to do this before the kids go to college and we're stuck for good." She met him, astonished and shaken: "God, what is it, Bartlett? What's the matter?" Perhaps understanding better than he did, perhaps because she felt some of the same things, she did not frame the questions.

Therefore he didn't have to answer; instead he tugged at her, pleading as though for her life. He could not at the moment have explained why it was so urgent, only that it was. He said, "Oh Ellen, I don't want to die before I've seen Europe. Please, let's take some time off and go on a trip."

This time she did speak, flushing with pleasure. "A trip? Oh Bartlett, I'd love to take a trip." In the next second, of course, it all came in on her. She jammed her knuckles in her mouth, managed to speak through them. "The money!"

"We'll find it. We have to."

"Bartlett, how can we spend so much?"

"The money doesn't matter, the only thing that matters is this." He rushed on, taking her by storm. "Ellen, I love you. I do, let's don't worry, let's just do this together."

She may have understood. "Oh God, Bartlett, what's wrong?"

"We're going to turn our lives around."

Which as much as anything explained why March found them in of all places the Soviet Union, Bartlett lying next to Ellen in heavily draped, baroque feather beds in Soviet hotels, surprised by restlessness because whatever the solution to his life, he had not arrived but was still moving toward it. In spite of the extravagance, the risk of trying again in new places, he was as he had been to Ellen and Ellen was the same to him. They were the same together. Loss clawed at him from the inside, the fact that he could not creep out of bed in the night and reach his love by telephone. At the Parthenon, in the Hagia Sophia, they were only Bartlett and Ellen, traveling through life as they always had done, side by side. Ernie would not even be jealous, but Ticia would.

Did you and she do things in all those places?

Anything I do, I want to do with you.

He wondered, was this true? Playing at being lovers, Bartlett and Ellen fell into the same old attitudes no matter how exotic the surroundings, or how strange the bed.

She did not go with him to Siberia, but stayed in Leningrad with the rest of the tour. He and three or four others went on alone and therefore when the train stopped at a tiny station in a snowy waste there was nobody to prevent Bartlett from wandering outside to marvel at the frozen plain, nobody to shout when, for the first time in this trip certain of what he was doing, he followed his heart, and strayed.

As he had hoped, the snow blew around him, obscuring everything. If he kept his back to the railroad, he was as good as alone. Within a few feet, he might as well have been. When the train whistle sounded it would take him a few minutes to re-orient himself; he would have to bend his head and hunch his shoulders, walking into the wind to get back to the others, but for the time being he could be completely on his own.

He cried out, whether for the absent wife or the lost illusion, the lackluster love or the brilliant lack, he could not have said. It was gone; he knew everything was gone. He howled.

Thus Bartlett J. Daniels, public servant, librarian, halted, arrested in the frozen territory with his jaws frozen wide, eyes salted with rime; he was for the first time in memory absolutely without shelter, spilled out of the enclosure of his obsession, naked and riven, yes—God! He was going to have to do something about his life.

The Protective Pessimist

Intimations of doom may be no more than a prickling at the back of the neck, a pervasive, sourceless dread that could be passed off as anxiety, or paranoia—the need never to be taken unaware. *I told you something was going to happen.* Thus Sarah, in any given situation: Sarah, the protective pessimist. *I knew there was something wrong.* For a certain kind of woman, the need to be on top of things outweighs the horror at turning out to be right. She is never disappointed and she is sometimes pleasantly surprised.

The disaster first manifests itself as rustling, as of leaves turning in the wind; sand and small objects race along the roads—flecks of sourceless, stinging debris. As the wind grows stronger, a shadow rushes across the earth, flushing small creatures and sending them scurrying before it. Hurry; danger, *danger*—but—what? There is a disturbance in the hedgerows: things—no, people—running in the culverts, carrying what they can because it is clear the world is ending, and if they must go they will not travel empty-handed into the void.

Her old dream: A landscape such as this one, with dust whirling in the road and the racing shadow devouring the land; with up ahead, the black sky turning an unearthly green. In the dream she had read, or heard, the rest: WHEN THE BEAUTIFUL LADY USES *THIS*—all right, under her arms—THREE TIMES AND

GOES TO SLEEP BETWEEN FLOWERED SHEETS, THE
WORLD WILL END. A stick deodorant against the apocalypse?
A stick deodorant. Mennen's Lime. Could she really bring it
on?

If this were a "Twilight Zone" the car would break down about
now, and she and Bruce would be taken in by a spooky old
householder. When it became clear that they were not going to
get out of here tonight, she and Bruce would take a flashlight up
to bed, and the sheets. . . . It was only an old dream with no
deep underlying symbolism, merely a nocturnal disturbance
brought on by—what was it Bruce had said when she tried to tell
him about it? Robbed it of all dignity, saying: "Something you
ate, probably—an undigested piece of meat." All these years
later she could not shake the dream. It always came back to her
in this time of year and in these circumstances. For one, two,
several years she would forget and then she would be going
somewhere in the car; Sarah was always the passenger when
this happened, looking moodily out the window at this precise
hour; they would be going along in the bare, gusty dusk of early
November, in the week before all the leaves let go.

Now. Something is going to happen now.

This could be only a personal feeling of creepiness, Sarah
thought, resting her forehead against the glass. But there was
that disturbance in the bushes as they passed IBM headquarters, and up ahead she saw papers—as if from an attaché case
cracked like a nut, with its contents scattered in the road. There
was a man in a three-piece suit wearing a homburg and carrying
a London Fog raincoat, walking determinedly along the shoulder on the opposite side of the parkway, with a grim face turned
wherever he might be going.

Bruce said, "Wonder where he came from?"

She answered too quickly. "Car probably broke down." She
already knew that there was no abandoned car. The walking
executive had been cracked out of his office today like a living
oyster out of its shell. He would have been at his desk in one of
the many corporate headquarters that flanked the parkway,
veiled from the eyes of passing drivers by tastefully sited ever-

greens. Ordinarily he would still be at work. He had left early and on foot—not without a fight. What had befallen him? Where was he going now? He had managed to get out with his hat, the coat, and in the attaché case, all his appurtenances. He would have put in his desk calendar, cards wrenched from his Rolodex; his pictures of the family in their silver frames and certain crucial manila folders. Did they know about the missing files, and would they come after him with dogs? Was he an industrial spy? He would have run along the rows of boxwood like a clever fox; she admired his dignity, even in flight. He was going along at a brisk pace with, she thought, a self-deprecating set to his mouth: *Could have happened to anyone.*

This was an area of vulnerability she did not choose to inspect.

"When I have my memorial service," Bruce said, "I want a Dixieland band and an open bar."

She said, with malice, "Open coffin?"

"I want to be cremated and flushed down the toilet," Bruce said.

"If you died, I would die." This seemed to strike a wrong note so she went on hastily, "I think I would like to be sewn into a canvas bag and buried in the garden."

"Do you want the kids to dig before the ground freezes?"

"Not so fast, Abernathy."

It seemed to her that there were businessmen standing at every outdoor phone stall in the next rest area they passed. They were all too well dressed for the roadside rest stop, making calls in London Fog raincoats or in some cases Chesterfields (a little early in the season), consulting phone lists and making hurried notes on pads. Somebody had explained to her that office phone rates were so high that businesses found it cheaper to send their men out with pockets full of quarters or, she supposed, a company credit card. There was, however, the possibility that they were victims of the same disaster that had left the man with the attaché case quivering like a newly shucked sea creature, naked before the elements for the first time in his life. What would become of him now that he had no place to go in the mornings? What if he got to his house and the little woman had changed the locks? Gone would be the three squares and the extensive credit line. He would have to wreak sustenance from the earth. He would learn how to sleep wherever he fell. For a while he could steal from the wives of Westchester, but eventually he would have to learn how to hunt and trap.

What disaster had overtaken him, and was this only the beginning? Aliens from another planet might have done this, insinuating their number into high places until they reached critical mass. This must have happened some time this morning. All over Connecticut, executives would have gone into board meetings to encounter similar salutations. They would or would not get explanations. "Gentlemen, this may come as something of a surprise to you, but your company has been taken over by several of our number. You have four hours to clean out your desks."

She wondered whether the mask, or shield, the aliens had created to make themselves look like businessmen had dropped, now that there was no longer the necessity. She would have liked to know whether, leaving the boardroom, the businessmen looked back. Did they see giant fish or unimaginable gelid things or stereotypical scaly monsters waving tentacles lazily as they occupied the paneled boardroom, and did they escape with dignity or did they scream? Maybe the enemy looked exactly like them: pink and freshly shaven, a little plump just above the collar, where the shirts were growing too tight for the badly toned flesh of the neck.

The memorial service Sarah and Bruce had gone to New Haven for was a model of its kind; all those faces they had known as newlyweds, marshalled to make the appropriate gestures over one of their number who had, unforgivably, succumbed to time. As the places of childhood seemed smaller when a person went back to them, so did these people at Battell Chapel. Meeting the couples who were, say, ten years older, Sarah had found herself unhappily alert to ridges on the fingernails, the telltale rings around the neck. As a kid from the boonies all those years ago she had thought of these people as holding the keys—if not to life, then to a certain kind of knowledge. Now their mouths quivered as they spoke to her; without wanting to, she saw their nails had yellowed. Tightening her muscles in her own neat body, she noticed which of the women had let their bellies and behinds go to jelly and which had fallen away, what the hair looked like after all these years. To her shame she noticed which ones wore woolens discolored by too many dry cleanings. It seemed urgent to create or recall charms against whatever force had gotten hold of them. *Not going to let myself get. . . .* Not going to let.

Leaving the city to come up here, they had passed a kid on what looked like a burning bicycle, although, bemused, she thought now it might even have been a burning kid. As she watched he careened into a gas station and leaned the thing against one of the pumps. She could not know what had happened after she and Bruce pulled onto the East River Drive. Did she hear the boom of a distant explosion? If she looked back, would the sky over 96th Street be red? For Sarah the world was always ending, and always more or less this way.

Now, rolling home down the Merritt Parkway, she saw two more businessmen walking along the verge. There might have been a third and a fourth crashing out of the bushes at a dead run. What had overcome them, she wondered, that had turned them out on the roads at this hour, when it was too early to leave work and too late for a stroll? Jogging suits might have made it all right. They might, of course, be walking away from the rest area where the members of their carpool converged and dispersed, but there was the matter of the time, which was all wrong, as was the light. . . .

It was almost green, like the light in the. . . . Too often when she felt disconnected or threatened in some way, Sarah fell into the remembered dream of herself in the hedgerows, running ahead of the apocalypse. She had never been able to see the end of the dream, but the constant was: precisely this light.

If not displaced by aliens, she thought, perhaps these men were dislodged from their offices by an enemy closer to home. The women had come out of their cubbyholes and their kitchens and moved inexorably across Westchester like army ants. They might not be as strong as some of the men, but they were often smarter and usually more persistent. Given enough time, they could destroy anything. The displaced executive should have been more alert to small signs this morning: the wet newspaper on the surface where he fixed his breakfast, the rancid orange juice the wife had left for him, the hairline crack in his breakfast egg. Called to the boardroom like all the others, he would be confronted not by aliens in business suits but by a bevy of women in exotic costumes, from camouflage suits to sequins—conquering women, looking exactly the way they liked to think of themselves. *You should not wonder that this is happening, only that it has taken us so long.*

Was this a local phenomenon or was the upheaval universal? Were there similar refugees in every capital untouched by civil war or famine? In Tokyo the women would make their move with the force of Sumo wrestlers; scuttling, the menaced executives would seem to shrink. From between this one's ribs would protrude the geisha's hairpin; that one would flee the hari-kiri knife.

The return to New Haven for the funeral had exposed a large area of vulnerability. Usually Sarah could imagine she and Bruce were safely out of it—removed to the city for a change of life. Their friends in the city were younger than they were, and didn't know it. At least she thought they did not. It was a subtle point but she knew you didn't have to get old if you didn't feel like it. This worked most of the time, but there was always a problem with people you had been young with. If they looked better than you did, it was depressing. If they looked less good, it was worse. Like her own children, old friends became yardsticks, measuring her off.

"Where do you think they're *going?*"

"Who?"

"You know. That I keep seeing. Along the road."

"You mean the guy whose car broke down."

"What if something terrible is happening?"

"Nothing terrible is . . ."

He didn't have to finish. She recognized the tone. "Maybe I should start night classes. Or get another dog."

"That would be almost as bad as having another baby," Bruce said.

"I know."

"I wish I knew what you were really talking about."

She thought, but did not say, You always used to know. She felt like one of those small animals running before the shadow; if the late afternoon light was green now, and she could not control or even identify the source of her foreboding, then that which the dream foretold might be near. It occurred to Sarah that it might be a purloined letter situation; that the trouble wasn't in the bushes, or on the verge, but in the car. It would be too bad if the dream she had carried all these years turned out to be about something as pedestrian as getting old.

But the businessmen: something unexpected was happening out there in the woods beyond the Merritt Parkway. It crossed her mind that the upheaval might be the result of a prodigious feat of brainwashing in Korea, thirty years ago. All those released POWs had come back to the States with a buried agenda. Now that the signal had been given, anything could happen. Whatever the enemy planned would now be realized.

Bruce said, "I thought Mason looked terrible."

"He's not in shape."

"None of them are in shape."

"It would have been kinder of Bill to die in the spring," she said.

Bruce reached for her hand. "I know."

There were not very many cars on the road for rush hour. What if the refugees were commandeering them at the exits? Would there be skirmishes and chases at the Triboro Bridge? Once they got back to Manhattan they could duck into a subway, and be safe, but safe from what? What if the things that were going to get them, or the people, were waiting at the 96th Street exit? What if they came into the lobby to find them crouching over the body of the doorman: woman conquerors with no sympathy for collaborators, or was it aliens, or brainwashed businessmen? If it turned out to be the army of women, Sarah might be rehabilitated, but what would become of Bruce? They had fought side by side too many times for her to turn her back on him, no matter what the women said.

Every trip to the old hometown in South Carolina had cemented the bond. Sarah and Bruce against the past. Would they stand shoulder to shoulder against the future? She did not know. Going back was not something they liked; aging parents made it a necessity. They tried to protect themselves on those home visits, but too often they were thrown into the old circumstances. Childhood friends expected to remain friends, which was reasonable except that no matter how carefully they dressed or how hospitable the light, she would be forced to look into their faces and count the lines. Not yardsticks. Mirrors. Going back to the hotel, she would forestall an honest answer, asking Bruce: "Do we look like that? Tell me we don't look like that."

"No, of course not." It was her place to raise such questions and his to pass them off. "We are never going to look like that."

Once in South Carolina they went to a party given for the next generation by the mother of a high school friend. As teenagers they had necked in this funny, frivolous little woman's living room while she was at work. In the kitchen her son would be making tuna fish sandwiches because, though she had a certain homely chic in her jersey dresses and red high heels, she was never any good at food. Now her granddaughter was getting married, which meant Sarah and Bruce were old enough to be . . . . Not really. People said: "You must have been a child bride."

Today at the memorial service she'd felt more or less safe, but at the Boat Club in South Carolina she had not felt safe. In that territory people lay down with generations of their past and their entire present, with the future implied. There were three generations in that room—all the remaining fathers; the mothers, who like their hostess were still well turned out in pastels; their own contemporaries, including their friend Arthur, the father of the bride; their friends' kids. Perhaps because their own three would not be caught dead there, she and Bruce could be the kids. They spent most of their time at the party with their friends' children, who had the kind of vitality Sarah felt even when she looked in the mirror on a bad morning. They were all potential. Something drew them to Bruce and Sarah—was it northernness? Energy? When she and Bruce were in high school here, the parents of these people had shimmered in just this way. Between then and now something had happened to them, but what?

Looking at the hostess, whose New Year's Eve parties at the Boat Club she and Bruce had crashed as teenagers, Sarah understood that it was only a matter of time before the third generation put on the same bright expression, to hide. . . . Everybody got drunker sooner than they'd used to, which was bad. Everybody's parents had aged, which was to be expected, but now their contemporaries had aged. Sneaking out early to put on shorts and go to the movies, she and Bruce were certain they had more in common with the young.

Not like that. All their lives they would collude in youth.

In a way it was sweet, watching their old friends turn into their own parents, seeing this generation's children preparing to become them. There was the restfulness of the expected, the consolation of continuity. The past, the present and the future were all there in the graceful room with the yellow walls and the long white windows overlooking the river. Everything any of them might need was there, along with everything any of them might become.

No wonder Bruce had been wild to get away.

There had been one particularly bad thing.

It was summer; everything was pretty; so was everybody—Arthur's mother the hostess, and her granddaughter; Arthur, their smiling high school friend. In his middle-aged way Arthur looked handsome in his white dinner jacket, less worried at getting old than proud to have a brilliant married daughter on his arm.

"Well Arthur," Bruce said falsely, "You haven't changed a bit."

"You too," Arthur said to both of them. Good lord, what if he was lying too? "Neither have you."

That was not the worrisome thing. Passing through the receiving line she had understood that the chic, homely woman of their youth was held in place by convention and propped by her son because her brains had blown out her ears; the smile was vacant, the gracious conversation no more than social reflex, perhaps the last thing to drop out when some cruel force turned her into a shell.

Invasion of the Body Snatchers. I wish.

Just north of the Greenwich tollgate there were police cars and a big, glossy sedan pulled up on the hilly shoulder. Right there in the grass two sportsmen were eviscerating a deer that had been killed by a car. Would they tie the antlers to the hood of their Mercedes as soon as the state trooper finished writing them up? It seemed to her the wind was not necessarily swifter, but somehow sharper today. It was still early but almost dark. *God take care of the wandering and the homeless on a night like this.* God take care of me.

What was going to become of the poor businessmen, she wondered. Would they wander off into the woods and die, or were they going to converge around wood fires tonight, gathering in hastily assembled camps? It might take months for them to find each other in the wilderness, but unless they did, there would be no coming back. She hoped they could survive the lonely weeks, the months of privation before they recovered themselves and began to regroup. In numbers, there might be strength. Making raids on the surrounding householders, they could stockpile food and arms. If they were smart they might begin to farm. If they were not too weakened by hunger and diminished by hardship, they could even mount a counterrevolution and resume their places. Would this be a good thing or a bad thing? She did not know.

It was a relief to be back in the city, to be leaving the car and going up in the elevator with plans for a comforting carbohydrate supper changing the light inside her head from green to gold. Food equals love sometimes, she told herself, thinking about fettucine and French bread. It had been a hard day, of which this was the hardest part, but at least she had come unscathed into the elevator in spite of the signs and wonders on the road. The rushing wind had abated, the racing shadow had diffused to become night; the small animals were already safe in their burrows. She and Bruce would console themselves by eating white things.

Inside the front door, hanging up his London Fog raincoat and standing squarely on one of the black diamonds in the foyer, Bruce said, as if he had been thinking of it ever since they got into the car outside the Lawn Club: "Sometimes I wonder if we ought to get a divorce."

The wind stopped rushing; she shuddered to a halt. *That miserable dream.* Maybe this was what they had been exceeding the speed limit to get to; maybe this was what the fleeing businessmen had been trying to tell her the whole time they were going along the parkway, or was it rather an advance warning, that allowed her to prepare without knowing what for? "Oh Bruce," she said, without even a pause for thought. "Where would you go?"

"You have a point there," he said. "Do you want me to move the car tomorrow morning, or will you?"

Fourth of July

I am so deathly afraid of those women.

Strawberry pie again, Eleanor, how nice. Pity it didn't set.

Every Fourth of July I vow not to, but sooner or later I sit down and cry. I used to cry the minute Philo came in the kitchen with the strawberries; he would start to hull them, thinking it was the work I was crying about, having to make seven pies. For the life of me I couldn't make him understand. "Come on, honey," he would say to me. "It's only my family."

No matter how early we start for the camp on the island we always get there late and they are all down on the dock waiting, his brothers and sisters and their families, all those blunt Maine faces in one place at one time, all those watery Goodman eyes, those huge Goodman women watching: Philo's sisters Marge and Edna, standing foursquare with Ralph's broad wife, Benjy's bride.

Oh Eleanor, strawberry pie.

When they all know his sisters won't let my bread on the picnic table, and only blood relatives get to make the beans. I begged them to let me bring potato salad but Benjy's wife Lane gets to do it, that hasn't been in the family half as long as me. Everybody else does such a good job that there are never any leftovers, but the pie comes last, and there's no telling with pies. Either something goes wrong with the crust or the filling or else

I get them almost perfect and something happens, people rush out or get too full to eat them and I have all those leftovers reminding me there is something the matter with the way I do things and all the way home Philo grumbling; I hate the pies.

They look lovely, Eleanor. Too bad Randolph couldn't be here, but I suppose in his business. . . . Well Randolph is in New York and it's hard for him to get away, you know these actors; they don't. *How come we never see him on TV?* Then one of those big old girls sighs and says, "Pity Evvie can't be here."

What they mean is, Poor Eleanor, all those years and nothing to show, when our own sons bring their wives and all their children. They would come a thousand miles to be with us. Every Fourth of July there is another grandbaby when all you have is poor Evelyn that Philo won't even let us mention in his hearing, and that fancy boy.

Last year Marge was scraping leftovers into the garbage; she stopped what she was doing for a minute, so dreamy I don't even know if she heard what was coming out of her mouth. "You know, your girl Evelyn's been gone for so long I don't know if I remember what she looks like. Oh Eleanor, my boys ate so much they didn't have room for your lovely pie."

Well I remember what she looks like. They sent for me from that terrible place in Augusta when she had the operation after her secret baby died. I had to tell Philo I was having my insides photographed, and then I had to go and have it done, so it wouldn't be a lie. He said, "My sisters never get sick," but he didn't mean to criticize. He was only wondering why bad things come to some but not to others, as if you could prevent all kinds of trouble if you only put your mind to it.

Strawberry pie again, Eleanor, how nice. I can hear them this very minute. I help Philo up on the dock and then I have to get the hamper. Wish I could drop the filthy thing into the water and jump in after it. *Oh look everybody, it's Eleanor, and she's brought the strawberry pie.*

"Poor Philo, if he hadn't married Eleanor. . . ."

They think I don't hear them. They think it's my fault Philo is so feeble. They think he should have married somebody big and strong, that knew how to take care of things—as if failure crippled, not age or disease. Two of Marge's boys help him onto the dock and I know that for the day at least he will be taken care of. Then I bend down for the hamper and my dress rides up in the back so they can all see clear up to where my stockings roll. When I pop up with the basket one of those big boys will be gawking; I see Edna's Milt looking snide as I hand up the pies.

Forty-two years of crying on the Fourth of July. That's six weeks of crying on that day alone, never mind the other times when I'm safe at home. I have to go off somewhere so they won't see I'm down; otherwise his sisters will be all over me, all fleshy farmers' hands and watery brown eyes.

Why Eleanor, what's the matter

What on earth's the matter, Eleanor

I know they mean well but there are so many of them with those same eyes, and after all these years I am still scared of them. I have to walk softly among them so they won't smell the fear on me and strike.

When I met Philo we were a thousand miles from here and I thought he was what I thought he was. How was I supposed to know he was only the tip of something larger, that big family with their big frames and the big hearts that he keeps throwing up to me. How could I know I was going to shrivel in their presence, when I was supposed to measure up? Only little Benjy came down for the wedding; the rest of them were planning a great big wedding party at the camp when Philo brought me home.

They were already on the island when we got there. The Goodmans are scattered over three counties and they might even seem ordinary when taken separately, but when they come together on that island they are enormous, like a bunch of bones that have snapped in place to make a dinosaur. They all come with hampers and casseroles and baskets of fruit and early vegetables and homemade pickles and preserves; they come loaded down with food nobody could ever finish eating, not even the whole state of Maine, because overflow has always been part of it, which is one of the reasons I always cry. I don't have much of anything to spare.

We sat down at trestle tables in the cabin Philo and his father and brothers made, everybody laughing and elbowing on the long benches, muttering over their food. They had gangs of kids pushing each other off benches at the children's table and smearing wedding cake. I could see the Goodmans were caught up in their own plenty and at the same time they were watching, judging me; the next thing I knew tears were running down my nose into the macaroni salad and I ran away. Philo flew up and followed me down to the dock; he was scared to death something was wrong. Then when I tried to tell him he pulled back and said, "Is *that* all."

I said, "I can't."

He put his arms around me. "It's only my family."

And didn't I bellow then. "I *know*."

He was all There there. "You'll feel better about it next year. Next year you'll have something to bring."

He meant the pies of course, somebody at the top of the world had decided what I was going to bring.

And I sobbed harder because I will always hate making pies but all those strong women will go to the grave without knowing it. And ever after he hugged me and went, "Sh sh, there there," I kept on crying because I already knew without knowing that no matter what I brought, it would never be enough because I am only the one person and together the Goodmans are that huge living thing.

When my Evelyn was born I thought: Maybe this will make the difference. Philo took care of her for two days that summer while I dragged myself around the kitchen making those hateful pies, I'll never forget all the paper plates with the leftovers still on them, going into the trash. Evvie was only four weeks old and I wasn't quite myself; Philo's brothers Ralph and Benjy had to help me out of the boat and then his big sister Marge looked into the blanket and I could just see what she was thinking when she said, "Oh look everybody, it's a girl." Then she put the blanket back because Goodman women only ever had boys, and I cried for embarrassment, for my baby Evelyn. They all brought presents, pink this and ruffled that. They said, "It's so nice to buy something pretty for a change," but I knew what they meant. Philo's Pop was still alive and he held Evvie in his two hands, weighing her against all those Goodman boys; she was next to nothing in his hands. Philo, he didn't see it; he idolized Evvie, he always did, which is why when she got to high school and went so bad, he took it so hard. He was tickled and dizzy that summer, rattling around the camp like one of them, but I could see their eyes when they thought I wasn't looking, and I knew.

One year Benjy's wife Lane took me aside. She'd been in the family for a while by then; all those Goodmans took right to her, good big girl, gave them lots of little boys with those big heads. I remember my sweet boy Randolph was hiding up in the woods where they all chased them, them savage cousins with their big shoulders and their tufted heads; he just hid and he wouldn't come down until night when all the other boats had left. My Evelyn was leading the pack that badgered him, filthy and loud as any of the boys, so it wasn't our poor Randolph I was crying for but Evvie, because she thought she was just as good as all the rest of them, the Goodmans with their shaggy heads and their big klunky feet.

At the end Benjy's wife came up to me, her voice was low and kind of There there, "These picnics are hard. Everybody feels the strain."

I looked at her and I thought: Potato salad, practically fool-proof; they all made a big fuss over it even though she and Benjy hadn't been married half as long as Philo and me. "Your salad was real good this year."

"Don't cry Eleanor." She was looking up into the dark pines, where Randolph had disappeared to, and I thought I heard her muttering, "I hate it," so we almost talked, but then one of the big boys jumped Evvie and by the time I pulled her out of the fight and got back to her, Benjy's wife was saying, "I'm always scared to death it will turn out mushy," and her boys were bouncing on her, she was surrounded by big strong sons, so I couldn't be sure what she'd really tried to say.

The next year we went to my family for the Fourth of July. I saw to it; I made Philo explain to his folks, he was sweet about it but the kids had fits when they found out; they whined the entire way. When we got there the house seemed too small and there wasn't enough food because my mother wasn't used to fixing for armies and there weren't any cousins so the children fussed the whole time. In the middle of it we had to call the camp and Philo and the kids had to talk to all the Goodman aunts and uncles and cousins while my mother and I sat at the empty table and tapped our fingers because we'd worked so hard and it had gone so fast and there was nothing to do but sit and listen to them phoning and look out the window at the rain.

Philo was sweet about it, he said we could go there every Fourth as far as he was concerned, but I could see his whole body twitching; it was like watching the shad fighting their way upriver to spawn; when his family gets together he has to be part of it, no matter who cries or what goes wrong they all have to come together at certain times.

We had wedding parties at the camp, first Marge's oldest, then Edna's, then Ralph's; Evvie was big enough to flirt with all the groomsmen and later on I guess she went up in the woods with more than one; I was ready to let it go by because I didn't want to know for sure, but the others wouldn't just let us *be*, they were watching like vultures on a branch, and they found out at the party we had when it was Ralph Jr.'s turn and we gave him and the girl a big to-do at the camp, Goodmans always say Waste Not Want Not so naturally we had it on the Fourth.

I brought the pies that year, there are two dozen different ways a person can spoil a pie, but that time they came out fine, wouldn't you know we had cake too, Marge made it along with the beans even though I said she didn't need to, we had plenty of pies. It was a big sheet cake with a bride and groom on top and Ralph Junior Plus Betsy in beautiful green script with so much butter cream frosting on top and so many yellow-and-green butter cream rosebuds that nobody had much room for my pies.

Even so the first part of the day was sweet; Philo's parents were gone by that time but one of the nephews and his wife Teeny had brought a brand new baby, and that poor new mother spent the afternoon running back and forth with baby bottles and heated jars of baby food while all the aunts snuggled the sweet thing with big smiles on their big faces and the young people just drifted off, some of them this way and some that. We all said all the usual, how big all the kids had gotten, how well everyone looked, it was a little like the opening responses that we go through on Sundays at church, a pleasure and a comfort when everything else is sliding and it's hard to tell who's who and what's what. When suppertime came and the light changed Marge and Edna and Benjy's wife and I all fussed over the trestle tables, setting places and laying out serving dishes; I remember thinking we were murmuring together like real kinfolks, even though I probably knew the big boys were up there in the woods torturing my poor Randolph; he used to come back to camp panting and bruised or bleeding from unexpected scratches: It's nothing, Ma, but pretty soon he'd skulk into some corner and hide behind a book until the day was over and we could get in the boat and go. My Evvie was off God knows where with the young people—Ralph's son the bridegroom and his friends, that girl he was marrying tried to pretend she was busy with Teeny's baby but I knew. When Evvie came back she looked drunk but the young men were showing off and making fools of themselves over her so I didn't say anything about her blouse popping and her bra straps slipping; I thought: for once we are all in the middle of things.

Then dinner came, music and noise and firelight on the rafters; we ate inside because it was cold on the Fourth that year. One of the boys said something to Big Ralph and he whispered to Philo. Then I saw Philo get up from the table, shaking, and I can't tell you now if it was anger or if God had struck in that instant and this was my first warning: maybe I was supposed to be expecting the stroke he had in September, and the palsy that followed the stroke. He got up before we even had the cake, trembling Philo in the wake of his oldest brother, stumbling toward the woods. They brought her back down along with the young man, who was he, some friend of Ralph Junior's that his wife was sitting right there; I could hear Philo yelling and hitting and Evvie shouting while we all sat and ate that wedding cake and pretended not to hear anything, and everybody got so full on cake that I had to take home all my pies, but I can tell you I waited until we got halfway back to the mainland and dropped them over the stern; Philo was so mad at her he was still shaking and I can *not* begin to tell you what I was thinking when I said, into the sound of the motor churning, It serves you right.

My Evvie was gone before the Fourth came around again. She used to send me post cards care of Marge, Philo's own sister, imagine, and I would slip off to see her whenever she was in Augusta, even Boston, I always got there but I always had to lie because nothing is that simple but I know Philo blames her for the stroke.

When the family gets together now somebody always gets me aside and asks, but off somewhere, so Philo won't know. I tell them she is working in a restaurant when it's a bar or worse, and that she is engaged when there are too many men; I told them it was pneumonia when whatever she had wasted her tubes so she can never have babies; they don't pry. I don't know why, but when we talk about Evvie, his sisters and his brothers' wives and I are almost close, whispering because Philo says she's as good as dead to him, he doesn't even want to hear her name. They always ask and I really want to tell because for once I can say my girl's name out loud and that brings her into the room with us, for a minute at least. I will say this for them, they have none of them ever blamed me for Evelyn, although I know they blame me for a lot of other things.

They probably think it's my fault Randolph turned out the way he did, something about the way I am that made him choose what he chose; between Evvie and Randolph my Philo is never going to have any grandchildren and in that family this is a big thing. They probably think it's my fault poor Philo is failing so;

he shakes so bad he can't go to his job at the post office, they've cut him off and pensioned him out so that part of his life is over, like so many things. He sits around home all the time now, in front of the TV; sometimes he shakes in my arms at night and I know what he's thinking: What did I do that brought this down on us; what was my big mistake? Then I start shaking too and gnaw the insides of my mouth to keep from telling him: You never should have married me, with my small bones and my skinny face, I can't even make a proper strawberry pie. Sometimes at night he bites my shoulder to keep from crying and he says, Eleanor, take care of me. Even if I can't do anything else, Philo Goodman, I'll always take care of you.

The pies didn't set this year either, but something new came along with us in the boat, nothing I could see but I knew it was there, round and real as an egg. It was not exactly hope but more of an expectation, because Evvie called this morning while Philo was in the bathtub, she said not to ask how but sooner or later today I was going to see her, we would hug and say hello before the night was out. So I carried that in the boat with us like an extra passenger, I was thinking she might walk in on the hot dog roast at noon, married to some nice farmer and happy at last, or else she'd come with a pot of beans in time for the big supper, she'd have her handsome husband with her and in spite of what the doctors said she'd have a baby in her arms.

Oh Eleanor. They were all on the dock, waiting. I thought I could read something new in their faces but all they said was, "Look everybody, it's Eleanor. She's brought her strawberry pies."

I don't know why but this time I bent down for the basket and I came up fighting, saying, "They're not *my* pies, Marge, they're *your* strawberry pies. If it wasn't for your family, I would never make another strawberry pie."

She pulled back with a look but she didn't say anything, she just handed the basket to one of her big boys, I guess it's grandsons by this time, and then Philo's big sister stepped over close and murmured, "Did you get a phone call?" But I was holding my secret call from Evelyn close in my heart; I would show them all, and in the next second so fast that I couldn't tell if the two things were linked she said, "Benjy's in the hospital. He won't be coming out."

"That's terrible."

But Philo came up complaining, where was Ben when he was needed on the Fourth, tests are one thing, but this is family, Benjy never cared for us he just . . . she threw me a look: Shall I tell him? I shrugged: he doesn't want to understand. He just kept on, so bent on it that she gave me another look: he would wait a long time before she'd be the one to tell him; he could rot in hell. And in that funny minute it crossed my mind that maybe it wasn't the family that expected so much from us at these gatherings, but only Philo, and at the same time I heard Marge's voice like a rosebud trailing down my arm: "You always did try too hard."

I was afraid I was going to cry or flare up because she'd found me out but the rest of them were waiting, all those stout Goodmans waiting to bow their heads over the food; I had to pull myself together for Benjy's wife Lane if for no other reason so I told that poor girl the only thing I could think of: "Your potato salad looks just wonderful."

Lane hugged me and we both managed to keep from crying. "So do your pies."

It was different at dinner, not just because Benjy was sick and I was watching the door every living minute, wondering was Evvie going to walk in or would she beckon me outside. Everybody was restless; the grandchildren were fighting and spilling milk, and Marge and Edna couldn't seem to keep still; they kept running over to the window, and I could tell they were distracted—something had gone wrong with the beans. Even Ralph's good old wife, who is fat and getting stiff, got up and went out in the middle of dinner: "I just can't get enough of the moon." She looked over her shoulder like a girl. Then she called Marge out to look at it and then Marge came back in while we were clearing the table for dessert; she said, "Eleanor, you've got to come out and look at this moon."

"My pies!"

"The moon, Eleanor."

This year my pies were perfect, *perfect,* and she wanted me to. . . . How could I go outside? But Edna had me by the other hand and they were tugging me along, "Come on, it's important," big old Goodman women nudging me along like woolly mammoths bumping or two kindly old mother bears when all the time I was jangling like a wire and my voice kept on going up, I couldn't help it, "You just don't want to have to eat my pies."

I don't know what I wanted: for them to agree or for them to fight, us women to have it all out in the open, whatever it is: why I come here year after year and in all these mortal years of human sufferings at picnic after picnic, their beans, our children, my poor pies, I'm still not one of them, I could hardly stand it but here they were, pulling me along. They just pulled me out the doorway, pointing to Philo and shushing because they didn't want me to know, they were moist and sweet as big old girls with a party secret. They took me down on the dock and pointed across the water to this spot in the dark that was a flashlight on the landing blinking: Off and on, off and on.

Marge said, "It's Evelyn."

Everything in me fell out. "Oh Marge."

"Come on," she said. "We can't let Philo know."

So now I am in the boat again but we're going in together, me and Philo's two sisters and his brothers' wives who have arranged this and kept it a secret from Philo because they know what he is like and they know what he would do, my poor grudging Philo who's never forgiven a hurt and never will. It's the Fourth of July again and of course I am crying but this time it's at our meeting, my girl Evvie's and mine, and after my Evelyn gets back in her car and goes away the rest of us will get in the boat together and go on back out to the island, and if I cry again it will be because we were always together, these women and me, only I didn't know.

The Garden Club

She knew she did it well, had done this well almost all her married life; she would spend days on it if she had to, just to make it right. Still, every time the members of the Garden Club came to Alicia's house, her mouth dried and her belly trembled.

Employed as she was now, for the first time in her life a working woman, Alicia understood she was suspect among the lovely friends of a lifetime, who carried their age lightly and chattered like girls. This made success here more important. She had to be good at life precisely because now she was good at work. It was as if each small gain in other areas increased her vulnerability, in some geometrically enlarged arena of risk. She did not so much court as create these moments of insupportable tension, which were only sometimes followed by a measurable triumph. It was necessary to win. Petty triumph, Alfred would have said. Well he was wrong.

They would be here soon. Spilling into the house, the girls would make a pretty spectacle: Janice and Gail, exotic Clarita, who had Spanish blood, and Elise. Alicia could hardly wait to see them, all those well-dressed friends of her marriage nodding and rustling in the slanting dust-flecked sunlight, with their nails bright and their hair enhanced by touches of bronze or gold. Murmuring, they would hug her, the living complement to her carefully designed rooms; then they would take off their coats and judge. Although they would have been astounded at the suggestion, competition was the air they breathed. Smiling, they measured each other off. Alicia looked forward with love and fear to the moment when they finished their sherry and clustered in her dining room, judging the arrangement.

For the arrangement was everything.

How could she make the football hang in the air above the miniature goal posts on her polished table, forever indicating victory: the means, or was it the emblem, eternally poised? How could she keep it in the air until they came? Could they tell from the way she used her blues that Yale was supposed to be the favorite? Would they know the roses symbolizing Harvard were overblown by design, to signify Harvard's defeat? Even fulfilling the Garden Club guidelines—centerpiece, Football Brunch—she wasn't sure she had it right.

"It's perfect," Alfred said when he came down at dawn today and discovered her in tears over the tottering goalposts, the unstable ball.

"It's not," she said, afraid God would hear and take everything away. ". . . Is it?"

"Everything you do looks wonderful to me," Alfred said indifferently, so promiscuous in his praise that she knew he didn't see.

"Something is wrong with it," she groaned.

"You shouldn't let these things bother you." He seemed pleased to find her worrying over flowers for once, instead of the job. "What are you doing?"

Her job! She was holding the phone book at arm's length, trying to make the numbers hold still. "Tad will know what to do."

"For Pete's sake it's Saturday morning! He's probably asleep."

"He's a runner," she told him with a proprietary thrill. "He'll be up."

Alfred's voice spiked in irritation. "Why didn't you ask me?"

"Because I knew what you'd say."

Of course Tad came, her young employer in his Saturday sweats soberly bending over the arrangement, never once suggesting even by inflection that this was a waste of his time. She leaned close, absorbed, as he did magic with a piece of wire. "You do good work," he said.

Alicia knew what he was too polite to say, that there were better places to do it, yet she did not so much suffer as encourage the Garden Club, traveling to Hartford for the special glass marbles, setting bachelor's buttons in washable blue ink overnight to enhance the color, getting up at five to arrange the fresh flowers, using her own breath to fog and polish the fruitwood table. If at her new job in the library she had to spend hours searching a title for some medieval scholar; if she could never catch up on the paperwork Tad and the other kids in their twenties seemed to toss off in minutes, she was still good at this. In the moment before they came, she could be perfect.

Alicia loved the way her house looked in the morning light, the golden promises of autumn in this near-perfect moment right before they came. It was her favorite time of year, and the saddest; everything was so pretty, its time so short. . . . She had dressed in rust today, to match the leaves; the committee would come in fall colors—Janice and Gail, Clarita and Elise, whose race memory, or sense of the appropriate, would direct their color choices as it had every October since they first went off to college, five tremulous, gawky girls. When they were standing around it, admiring, her arrangement would be complete.

Alfred was out raking leaves in old boots and a Shetland sweater; in a few hours she would hear cheering from the Yale Bowl as the crowd rose for the kickoff. Thirty years ago she and Alfred used to walk out to the Bowl with hundreds of others, lugging blankets and thermoses. She remembered her doctor in another autumn, waving at the open hospital window: Hear them cheering? By the time the game is over, you will have your baby. Yes it was a cliche. She loved cliches. Hence the arrangement.

She had begun to understand that there were in life challenges it was appropriate to meet and others it was better to avoid.

Within the circle of the Garden Club she still had the capability, as the computer people said, of fulfillment. At least she needed to tell herself this when, in fact, she understood—if she understood anything—that life had been created to demonstrate Goedel's Theorem of Incompleteness, unless Goedel's theorem was an analog for life—the hand forever reaching for the eternally receding cup.

You are too smart to sit home, her young boss had said after their first conversation, in the year she went back to school. She was not sure what he saw when he looked at her. Whether he had spoken out of admiration or pity she still did not know.

Alicia would have put it another way. Her children were grown. Her watercolors had dried up in their tubes, which was all right because in her new, apparently insatiable drive for excellence she understood that her paintings had never been anything more than ladylike. Abandoned when she gave up photography, her darkroom filled up with wintering plants. She could no longer be certain she was at the beginning and not the end of something.

Then one night she woke up screaming and felt Alfred gently trying to disengage his fingers even as he patted her back and murmured, from long practice, There there, Lissy, there there.

So she went back to school. At the university she had to run hard to stay in one place among swift, indifferent kids who did well precisely because they didn't need it. She used to go home exhausted while the kids, her classmates, ran around like jackrabbits, falling into bed with just anybody anywhere, any time, dancing if they wanted to, partying late into the night. Well let them. She was better organized. She took some assurance from her surroundings, or was it the setting she had created: the glinting prisms in her chandeliers, the polished surfaces of her ancestral furniture, feeding on her reflected image in the beveled mirror her great-grandparents had taken from New York to Baltimore in the back of a wagon. Standing in the dust-shot sunlight she thought she saw her own reflected face receding; I need to be useful, she told the image, *useful.*

When she blundered into the manuscripts library, stymied

by a graduate school assignment, Tad Elson was more than kind. Did she remind him of his mother or was there more? Although she preferred not to admit it, he had invented her, directing her thesis, creating a job for her. Well it was easy for him to make large gestures. *Everything is easy for Tad,* she thought resentfully.

Unlike Tad, she had to work long hours to accomplish anything. Unlike handsome, careless Tad, who had a small car and a girlfriend, she hated to go home. Still she could spend only so long at the library. When she got back to the house, no matter how late it was or how many lights she had left on, it would be empty and too dark. At least she no longer imagined she heard the voices of her grown children somewhere in the house. Howard was working for an oil company in Saudi Arabia and Martha was married and living in Florida with children of her own. Even in summer the house seemed cold and no matter how exhausted Alicia was, she would have to start dinner for Alfred, who had begun to affect a neglected air.

When it was all she did outside the home, Alfred loved her work with flowers. He used to come up behind her and put his arms around her waist, chin on her shoulder, admiring the arrangement.

When the kids were young Alfred had spent thousands helping her to complete her prizewinners—especially the one she'd wrought with her bare hands in the garage, using exotic jungle flowers and a vase from Sotheby's; she had replicated it in Bermuda to win the Grand Prize. She had made successes here; she had been photographed and written up. He had bought her a ring.

At the dinner table in those days Alfred would sometimes reach for her hand, in front of guests who smiled indulgently: "Lissy. Isn't she wonderful? The flowers!" He would pull her close when the company left, his face crushing her hair.

They were never closer than at those moments. Everything she did in those days was a credit to him.

At first he treated her graduate career like another extension or enhancement of himself, jetting to Europe to make a holiday of her scholarly errands, meeting her in the shade of some abbey in England or in Bonn for yet another honeymoon; couldn't he see she was serious? Re-creating herself, she began to argue at dinner parties like a bright teenager discovering her powers. Newly assertive, she found herself interrupting Alfred to tell the girls' admiring husbands about pigment on vellum, or cleaning incunables, and in thanks for support, she had dedicated her thesis to him.

She had surpassed the dear girls who were coming to her house today, her partners at innumerable bridge luncheons, loving givers of gifts at baby and wedding showers—by going back to school and taking a paying job. By having male colleagues, that she could have lunch with, Alicia had changed her standing among her friends, yet this created a puzzle: why should they judge her more harshly, precisely because she had accomplished more than they?

("If you work too hard you'll lose your looks," Elise had said once, quite gratuitously.

"Don't get so busy you lose track of your man," dark-haired Clarita said to Alicia before this old friend of Alicia's even had intimations that her own husband had strayed.)

But the girls had gotten together to give her a black-tie dinner party when she got her master's; when Tad gave her the job, they took her to lunch at the club. They were almost as pleased as Alfred. They had been college classmates, frantic mothers at a collective play group, who some years later discussed the loves and losses of their grown children with the same passion they'd had for their own; they were her friends.

Then why should her face ache and her shoulders twitch because they were coming up the drive? No matter how she tried to stabilize the miniature football it dropped to a vertical position, dangling foolishly over the clever teakwood goalposts she'd paid McBride to build. No matter how carefully she walked, the wretched thing quivered and tipped. Why should she think they wanted her to fail?

She'd read or dreamed she read about a transplant doctor in one of those bizarre weekly tabloids—a medical genius whose work on organ transplants was without peer. It was rumored that his taste for the delicate meat was such that he did the most exquisite of excisions—no scrap of inflamed tissue left anywhere because he was not so much ravenous as intoxicated by quality. Did he cook it right there, over a Bunsen burner in a corner of the operating theater, or did he like to take it home and eat it raw? Did he do this secretly, or did he offer bits to his resident, to the anesthesiologist? Did the nurses jump for leftovers, snapping like hunting dogs eager for a reward? Sometimes it seemed one way to her, at other times, another. Was he a figment of her imagination? She did not know.

She did know that anyone who aspired to success had to rise above detractors. If the doctor really ate the meat, then he probably deserved it. He had replaced failing hearts and kidneys with good ones, he was conferring life. He had a high function, an unassailable place in society. If she won the first round of judging in this category, let the women, walking away from the house, draw this picture if it pleased them: Alicia crouched in a corner, devouring baby's breath.

"Use a coat hanger," Tad had said—a serious scholar who cared enough to give her his time. "You can prop it with a coat hanger." Well this had almost worked. In some respect it had worked, because she would be able to say to the girls, "If the football wobbles it's my boss's fault. He came over at dawn today just to advise."

She wished the girls would hurry; it was only a matter of time before the goalposts listed in spite of the supporting marbles, and the whole thing began to slide.

Was Tad stifling laughter this morning, dutifully praising her work? Although he made a great show of being egalitarian he might despise her for having money, even as she would always secretly resent him for being young. She would never admit he had invented her, any more than she would forgive him for finding her weeping in the stacks that first day. Had he really seen promise in her, or was she his welfare work?

Useful. She couldn't remember whether he'd heard her say it aloud. Tad had pushed through her master's thesis to high honors in spite of the committee's complaints that Alfred's money bought trips other graduate students couldn't afford to make to all those museums and monasteries abroad. A good administrator, Tad needed to protect his predictions; he sent her to professional meetings, sometimes in his stead.

"Use initials when you publish," he said. "Your first name sounds a little—I don't know."

At parties Alfred boasted that his wife had been invited to give a paper in Kansas City or Quebec; once she came home late to find him standing in the kitchen, angrily stabbing his fork into an open can of beans. She had redeemed that one by producing the *pâté en croûte* she'd made and frozen against such eventualities—still the angel on the hearth, OK?

For a while she got up in the night to keep the kitchen immaculate, bought a cocktail dress in American Beauty rose because it made her look frivolous. She had to keep proving herself. In spite of his frequent presents and surprises, she still did not know; did her accomplishments make Alfred proud or angry, or did he need to keep her occupied, for reasons she could not divine?

She and Tad found it important to believe that he was not sorry for her and she did not envy him; that she wasn't really rich. Now that she'd almost finished creating herself, she found it necessary to dispute him in staff meetings, to argue over fine points of dating certain Books of Hours, even though he had hired her knowing that she would never really need a paycheck, not for food or lodging, not even for cigarettes or for the curator's wardrobe, in tones of prune and raisin, that she had bought to convince. She put on her new position like a costume, affecting a scholar's stoop. She would do anything to erase the housewife and dabbler, the woman she had been.

Leaving the manuscripts library promptly at five, Tad often looked at her with the assurance of a born careerist: "That doesn't need doing now." He might guess at the empty house, but he could not imagine the anxiety that kept her at her desk.

"You don't understand," she told him, "you've always worked. It's going to take me the rest of my life to catch up." If she fell short they would seize her liver; if she failed at this she deserved to have it eaten, down to the last delicious shred. It was Tad's fault that she had expanded her area of vulnerability. There were so many more things in her life now than there used to be, that she might do wrong. Going back to school she had imagined, rather, that she was covering the exits—the number of places where she put herself on the line.

This was the best: this moment before the women came, the light falling on the polished table in her silent house. When she felt ready she would bring the parts of her life together; she was going to dazzle her colleagues and the Garden Club with medieval illumination wrought in flowers—an illustrated capital, she thought, but at the moment she could not decide which letter she would choose. Once again, she would win the international competition, and Alfred—what would Alfred do?

Her most beautiful arrangement would always be *The Moon Walk*, conceived when her children were still young, with faces opening like flowers at her dinner table, in the uncomplicated days when she was primarily a homemaker, well before she enlarged the area of risk. This was before she became a competitor outside her local club, and she would always like it best because it didn't matter at all and therefore she had accomplished it with the careless grace of a Zen archer: a perfect iris curving from the perfect silver tube.

Accepting the trophy, she had never imagined that she would want anything more.

But they were here: the committee—Clarita and Janice, Gail and Elise, the friends—all right, the friends of her youth. She had drunk and giggled with these dear girls on the way to and from sorority meetings and college mixers and, in adulthood, in the car on the way to dozens of flower shows. They had cooked and dressed up for each other from the early days around the tiny kitchen tables in first apartments cluttered by small children's toys, through the years they had spent decorating gracious houses appropriate to their station, making festivities in spite of everything that happened to them, or perhaps because of it.

They had soldiered through cocktail parties at the Yacht Club and dinner parties without number, giggling on the sidelines at their children's weddings. They'd even managed to make a party of the luncheon after Clarita, the Castilian beauty, won her divorce.

It made Alicia proud to see them filing into her carefully kept house today: pretty and gratifyingly ageless in their autumn costumes, serene in the context of orderly households, successful grown children, exercise classes and clubs such as this one. It gave her a sense of well-being, of the order and fitness of life. She was rich beyond money: she had her place in the university library and yet she still belonged here. She loved the cashmeres and tweeds her oldest friends wore to her house, the muted lipsticks and nail gloss with which they honored her, the touches of antique gold.

"Lissy, darling."

". . . so glad to *see* you."

"So happy you came."

"Everything is just lovely."

It was; Ardena had cleaned yesterday while she was at work, and as they did so often now, she and Alfred had eaten out. So few things happened in the house on Friday nights these days that the nap on the carpets was still raised. The cut crystal glimmered and every fruitwood and mahogany surface shone.

"Lissy, you look wonderful."

She could see from their eyes that she did not. In a moment of schizophrenia she had accidentally mismatched the parts of her life. She had on her uncompromisingly grim raisin-colored curator's blouse with the disproportionately fussy skirt she'd worn to the last flower show. She didn't know whether the flesh on her shanks had fallen away since she began to live the life of the mind or whether it was her guilty imagination, but her pantyhose seemed baggy today, and, lord, her *shoes*.

"The arrangement, Lissy . . ."

"Oh girls, let's have sherry first."

They had always loved to gossip over a little drink. There was something wonderful about being together and looking marvelous; it gave them a sense of invulnerability, more: the illusion that they were still really girls.

In the old days before Alicia was tied up on weekdays, she used to travel with them to flower shows in exhibition halls as far away as Boston and New York; they liked to hire a limousine so they could . . . what was it Maud said? So they could let their hair down, chattering over a thermos full of Bloody Marys without worrying about who was going to drive, or whether they could make the train. They liked to top off the show with a three-hour lunch. They always did a little shopping in the best stores, encouraging each other to spend too much, and at the end of the afternoon they would command a shaker of Martinis for the return trip, laughing and leaning exaggeratedly as the limousine took gentle curves. Like a homesick child, Alicia wished for the pretty simplicity of that life.

Clarita was particularly beautiful today, in a cocoa suit with a peach cashmere; her hair was so exquisitely done that it was impossible to tell whether it was only frosted, or whether the frosting concealed grey. She had recovered beautifully from the divorce, took support from the fact that since the split she had thrived and triumphed, while her ex was already separated from his popsy, and miserable. Alicia had heard that there was a new man—somebody she had met on a cruise, but she could not tell from Clarita's expression whether this was true, nor could she read anything in Clarita's eyes. Her vision of Clarita was surrounded or overshadowed as if by a hologram: she had a completely different image of Clarita—as she had been when she found out her husband was leaving her.

It was in the spring that they were studying Japanese flower arranging at Clarita's house, using cherry blossoms flown in at vast expense from God knows where. Like most cruel springs it was extraordinarily beautiful; Alicia remembered touching blossoms, the polished pebbles, and not so much learning as *grasping* in an instant the complexity of the East. Was it six years ago? Eight? In those prelapsarian days things were not so much learned as known. She loved them all best as they were that lovely morning, five women, gracefully disposed.

How had they found out about Clarita's husband? Did she tell them or did they already know?

All Alicia could remember was sunlight and too much sherry, the women dreaming along until the surface fragmented, Clarita's pretty face distorting: "Some women—bitches—all they care about is that little *thing* hanging down." Alicia had heard or had not heard something, somebody . . . *clang*. Better get a job. Her mouth filled with tears, not for what had happened to Clarita but for the loveliness, the possibilities.

Last New Year's Alfred had carried her off protesting, took her away from work right in the middle of the week—he was going to keep her at the Plaza for three days; she imagined herself barefoot and cherished, wrapped in filmy gowns. Perhaps he was only being nice or maybe he was trying to turn her into something else, the silken wife; in bed he was like a desperate boy. She would always remember the lines and planes of the city as massed violet shadows, every vista an Art Deco illustration of something she'd never had.

Leaving the hotel to go back to their lives, Alfred had tucked her into a taxi as if placing something precious in a box; catching his expression of loving confusion, she was pierced by its sweetness—unexpected at this point in a long married life. She had opened her mouth to express—what? But he was already saying, *Better hurry, we don't want to miss our train.*

She was stirred. At the time she had been relieved to get back to the manuscripts library, where everything was safely past. At the office she could push her sweater sleeves above her elbows and keep her glasses on all day if she wanted to, hunched in the posture of concentration, just like all the other kids. When she had been at work for enough years, she thought, she could simply *be* this without having to think about it. She would be spared the interference of that nasty inner part that always pulled back like a camera, relentlessly recording: Alicia in costume at her desk in Medieval Manuscripts, assuming a pose.

It was recording now. The girls loved the arrangement, the most imaginative they would see today. They wanted Alicia to put on her things and come with them to judge the rest—didn't she want to change her shoes? Caught up in their laughter she would do this; coming down, she would hear and record indeli-

bly the fragmented, telling phrase: ". . . saw him with a . . ."
Who had said that in the flurry as they followed her to the din-
ing table? Clarita? To which of the others? Not to her. Probably
Alicia already knew, knew everything but the woman's name.

But her arrangement was the winner today. Laughing, they
would rush her out of the house, past the implicated Alfred,
who was still leaning on his rake, standing among the leaves in
his Shetland sweater; they would be gone in a golden whirl.
She had won this competition, yes, and if on Monday Alicia
found reason to fight with Tad over a point of scholarship, it
would not be because of what she had overheard, or already
knew; no. She was a serious medievalist. It was time for her to
come into her own.

She was like the doctor now, crouching over the lights and the
liver, extracting the last tantalizingly delicious bits; she had de-
veloped a taste. The arrangement was a success; the mono-
graph she was working on with Tad was going to become her
book, even if it necessitated a major rupture with him—after all
he was only a mediocre dabbler while she was going to be a
major scholar, just cutting her teeth on this first publishable
piece.

Clement

It's not Marti's fault he's put his elbow down in grape jelly, sliming his sweater, but he has.

We are too old to have children, Clement thinks, watching his blond sons bob at the breakfast table like dandelions just about to blow. They have big heads. Bowl haircuts are the best Marti can manage, and when the boys jiggle in their chairs and jump around like that, the hair shudders and stands straight out. Thomas, whom he named for good reason, and Michael, archangel from hell; we had them too close together. They fight all the time. His whole life now is yelling and mess and smeared cereal. Kids don't stop. You can't just put them down and say, There.

Mike pushes his brother, who pushes back. "Da-ad!"

I love you, but please don't.

"Guys!" He is looking at Marti, in the frazzled blue bathrobe, who does not look back; her pelvis let go when she had the babies; everything about his wife slopes downward.

Doesn't this bother you?

"His arm is on my side of the table."

"My arm was there first."

Arf arf.

The racket is killing me.

In high school he used to tear around drunk all the time; once he and Barty spent a night in Brother Frederick's office crumpling up Sunday *Globes,* all sections, until they filled the room; when the principal came to work Monday he could barely get in; Lord they laughed. Clement wants to hug his goofy little kids and roll them around on the floor like other dads until they giggle and shut up, but years of isolation have left him rusty. He wishes he could take lessons somewhere. Instead he hears himself yelling, "Cut it out!"

At the sink Marti sections his grapefruit serenely. His boys don't even look up.

They just keep sawing back and forth across the stamped vinyl table cover: He did/he did/no he did. The rooster pattern is scored by knife marks and rubbed white in places by Marti's attempts to keep it clean. Clement can feel grape jelly on the elbow of his sweater. "Did you guys hear?"

All he wants to do is read the paper. Tom bangs his cup on the table. Mikey giggles while behind his paper Clement pulls his nails through his hair, dragging scalp. "Marti!" When she responds automatically, murmuring, "Boys," which the boys ignore, Clement snaps, "I said, that's enough."

In the lost days Clement used to have breakfast alone at a carefully set table in the rectory; he read his newspaper and waited for the dishes to be cleared. He fed on the silence, and behind the morning paper he rearranged his face. It's as if he's been unshelled in a strange country where savages go naked and have no sense of right or wrong. If I can't even teach them *this.* Three and four and a half, both years short of the age of reason; dear Lord, he thinks, please let them get tired. He loves them, but it's hard.

They don't quit. "Aa-aaa."

God. If we were twenty, Clement thinks, but even twenty could not be amused by all this grot and confusion, the hard-knuckled blows and laughter that loses its breath and starts to shriek. "Marti, *please.*"

Take that. Mike bops his baby brother; Tommy's arm jerks and the milk flies.

Clement's fist hits the cluttered table. "Martha, in the name of God!" He is embarrassed by his anger but he just can't sit here any more. He misses their old selves. Crazily, he mourns for the roosters disappearing from the vinyl cloth. This is not what he expected: the constant disorder, the weary slant of Marti's back, the blue bathrobe matted where she leans against the sink. Do our meals always have to be this way? Please, if she would please just smile and sit down with him, but she can't. If their lives together are less than perfect, Marti holds herself responsible. She is after all, the woman who took him away from the. . . . Yes. Oh Marti, please don't. When anything goes wrong, his wife slouches around with that unbearable apologetic look: after everything you gave up for me. He knows it isn't her fault.

He knows as well that she is the decision he can never go back on. It is the nature of their situation.

She isn't like that with the kids. The smile she gives them when she turns is beautiful. "Oh, boys," she says without conviction. "Look what you've done."

Defeated, Clement flees the anarchy of the Saturday morning breakfast table, leaving the three of them mumbling contentedly in the rubble. He's ashamed of losing his temper with her but he doesn't know how to say so: *creak*. He's like the Tin Woodman, with his jaws clamped tight and nothing but an echo in his chest. Clem and Barty; oh, he misses those happy drunks. There's no way to read the paper now with his ears red and his hands shaking from the disruption. He's still not used to being so close—all these souls rubbing up against each other in this tiny house.

Listen, he didn't used to be what is it, uptight, but nobody says that now, him and Barty and the keg wedged in the back of the Corvette, bombing around in the boozy self-consciousness of kids who had overheard Father saying, "It's the ones you least expect that end up being priests." Laid out blind drunk and coughing up blood on some beach like Saul, who's caused such grief. . . .

Even in the living room Clement can hear them, too many particles piling up too late in his life. Although the kids sound happy now their voices are unremitting, and so Clement retreats to the patch of side yard where he can escape the racket and claim virtue, raking dead leaves out of the flower bed. He loses himself in repetition, and as he does so he escapes to the one place he can run away to without making himself look like a fool and beggaring their lives. It isn't running away, exactly. Not that kind of retreat.

At Montrose in the dawn of time he had his own room with only a handful of things in it: his books, the crucifix. Clothes. The days marched in order and the country nights were so quiet that Clement imagined he might even hear God. In the silences that year there was at least the possibility. On the hillside farm upstate each event logically followed: chapel, classes, study, work in the fields, more study, everything in the context of prayer; the routine alone was enabling. The freedom and security that order brings, Clement thinks. Everything designed to prepare the way.

At Montrose days unfolded in the light of the absolute. Clement still mourns the certainty. He misses the Latin mass for some of the same reasons; it went on in the same language in the same way, no matter what went on around you. And his classmates? He misses them, not now, but as they were then, when together, they believed most of the same things.

He and Barty Malone entered Montrose in the same year, along with Richard Preston, good Freddy and Hal. Clement could look into Barty's eyes and read what he himself was thinking; they were that close. The five friends had great hopes. They were going to be leaders, mystics, martyrs; God, they were babies, too young to know worse, all filled to exploding with passion for what they thought was going to be their lives.

A part of Clement is forever fixed in one singular night that first October; he can still bring back the crisp air, black trees scratching his window in the night wind. He heard a dog's bark like a gunshot ricocheting off the hills: Clement Duval flat on his back after lights out. What! It was like being shot. In one astounding second he was laid wide open, thunderstruck and left gasping, with everything inside him exposed.

Do anything to me, Lord. Anything. Just please do it now.

He gripped the edges of his mattress, trembling with excitement; it was like a sign from God, so abrupt that he took what he felt at that moment to be an intimation of the eternal, the fusion at the end of the world—Clement whole but transformed, everyone glorified, somewhere deep in the mind of God.

As soon as he could breathe again he lunged out of bed and fled it, colliding with Barty in the hall. Who snapped around with a sharp look, studying him: "What. . . ." Maybe Clement's pupils were spinning; he doesn't know what Barty saw. Squinting, Barty studied him, but after a minute he released Clement with a laugh: "Pax vobiscum, right?" and with a wacky wave Clement slipped back into the safety of Latin formula and ordinary friendship, responding: "Et cum spiritu tuo."

The next day he got up just like all the others and went on with his studies. He was no mystic, he knew. He was just going to have to soldier on. And did, for a long time. Years.

A lifetime later he is married—late. His two handsome, big-headed sons are squabbling in the kitchen, and returning from the safety of recollection, Clement has to wonder whether Marti ever regrets what they are trying to do here. Does she ever think of going back? They would never, really, because there's no returning after you've left, but does she ever go back in her mind? Some part of her must miss the time before, when none of this was even imagined and they were so sure.

But Marti is ten years younger, she grew up ten years short of the crashing certainty Clement remembers from parochial school—everything by the numbers, and you knew what the numbers were. When she started school, it was a whole new ball game. "It's a whole new ball game." That's what crazy Freddy said in Clement's living room five years after they finished at Montrose. By the time Marti entered the convent, questions were boiling over and she and the sisters were among the first to ask. This makes his wife more flexible, he thinks, Marti who slipped right back into jeans and big flowered tops and who gets down on the rug to tumble with the boys. Marti doesn't mind the risk and chaos kids bring; she seems better able to live their lives.

In the car coming home from the supermarket in late morning, the little boys wrap themselves around Good Humors and are quiet for a change. Getting out of the car Marti says, looking over their heads at Clement, "If you guys take naps after lunch, we'll have supper at McDonald's after church."

They'll have frozen pizza and ice cream when they go inside, and after lunch Clement is supposed to run the kids around in the park. He'll play tag and, short of experience as he is in dad stuff, he'll try to throw the ball around. Not knowing the frayed black topcoat gives him away, he thinks he even looks like the other dads. After he's worn them out he'll bring the boys back and Marti will put them down for naps. When it seems safe he and Marti will latch the bedroom door and lose themselves in each other and in their stolen, silky comfort, forget. What they do when they make love is both more and less than Clement's mysterious stroke of passion that night at Montrose. What he and Marti have, they have here, this afternoon, whereas what happened to Clement back then was all potential, raw, unformed Clement Duval transfixed in expectation, with nothing realized and everything still ahead.

But Marti's finger tickles his curled palm. McDonald's. "What do you think, Daddy?"

His blood leaps. "I think that sounds fine." Oh God, he thinks, I didn't marry Marti out of sexual weakness, I. . . . But his little boys are climbing him like a tree, clinging and rubbing him with wet mouths and soft faces, and it's all Clement can do to stay on his feet. Love makes him squashy. "Oh, guys."

"And maybe after supper we'll go to a drive-in movie," Marti says. It's cheaper than paying a sitter and in the spring the last remaining drive-in opens with heaters for the cars.

They don't have much money. On weekdays, Clement works as a guidance counsellor. Once a priest has renounced the power to say mass and administer sacraments, he has a limited number of skills. He's older than most of the staff at the high school but younger in experience of how the world works for these adolescents he's supposed to help or, for that matter, for a man who is no longer a priest. There is no rectory housekeeper to maintain life-support systems and screen visitors; he's shed the clericals which in themselves reminded others of his rank, or station, or—what was it—his anomalous position as celibate man of God.

I am more than my vocation, he thinks. He thinks he must be, but knows that when he left he lost more than his position in whatever is the heavenly holding pattern. He thinks: *I lost my job.*

Waiting for an answer, Marti is pink and slightly cross-eyed from trying to please him. "Unless you want to have somebody over for dessert."

Her finger in his palm: his mind is running ahead to love in the afternoon. He says stiffly, "I think a drive-in movie would be fine."

Clement was ordained early in June of 1968. In the garden at Montrose that afternoon, everything was in bloom; it was like the beginning of the world. Families juggled paper plates and plastic cups while nephews and nieces darted around the garden like paper airplanes, getting stuck in hedges and diving into the grass. Mothers and aunts and sisters all came to the reception in flowered dresses or pastels with flowered hats and in the dazzle of color and perfume. His sister Mona was already pregnant with her first; Clement saw ordinary life receding at lightspeed, like a planet he was leaving behind. Friends and families who could not quite encompass the changes in people they used to think they knew bowed their heads so the new priests could give their first blessings. While he trembled at the implications, Clement's own mother bent to kiss his hands.

Apart, he thought. I am truly set apart.

Only his classmates kept pace with him; he saw their excited, confused faces above the bent heads of their families. Clement didn't know. He thought he looked the same; he felt the same, but he could tell by the way his mother and even Mona treated him that he was no longer the same. At the end of the afternoon she hugged him but it was as if she'd forgotten they were friends. "Goodbye father," she said.

At the end of the day he and Barty ended up at the bottom of the lush spring garden: new priests, perhaps, men of God but still, by God, themselves. "Keep the faith," Clement said with a wry grin, and in loving irony Barty lifted one hand, sketching that Catholic kids' mock blessing, hail or was it farewell: "Pax."

By that time the Latin was done with; one of the prices they paid for change.

Of his first friends at Montrose, Richard Preston died of an embolism following knee surgery the following summer and Clement thought more than once how simple it had been for him—heaven assured. The rest of them were struggling through the Vietnam revolution, shaken by the storms that rocked the church into the seventies; in a body where faith was everything, the issue turned out to be sex and the catalytic question was about birth control. Unless it was conscience, Clement thought, or collegiality, or was it only change? Who would survive? As long as Barty was all right, he thought, they could both hang on. Hal joined the Berrigans in Baltimore and went underground; Freddy, who had begun by claiming acid was an aid to meditation, had ended in an ashram in India, leaving behind the outside possibility that he was right. To his grief, Clement understood that nothing was certain except that he was still a priest and in spite of doubt and dissent and confusion, so were the others.

Marti slips into bed beside him, silky and warm.

"Oh, my dear." He turns to her, thinking: This. I have not left heaven behind, I'm just going by a different road. He is prepared to lose himself, but as they embrace they are both aware of noise in the back bedroom where the boys are supposed to be napping and his hand on her belly freezes while they wait for it to subside. Considering his wife in the golden light filtered through the old-fashioned window shades, Clement thinks Marti never looks at home in anything she puts on because she's at her most beautiful this way. But the boys' voices get higher and louder; as the shouts and thumping start, his back and shoulders tighten. Maybe younger men aren't so easily bothered, but he was too old to get married and he's in his fifties now. Marti's hands are still moving; if she can she will keep him safe in their shelter of blankets; with her bare hands she will keep the rest of the world away—no use. The shouting turns into screams of rage and their sons' pounding shakes the bedroom door. "Mom," they are howling between sobs,

"Mo-o-o-m."

Clement grabs for something to cover himself so he can go out and deal with them, but seeing his face, Marti shakes her head, mouthing: *I'm sorry.*

"It's not your fault."

But there is that look: *mea culpa.*

Slipping on shapeless sweats, she lifts her voice. "Now you boys stop that."

Their voices could cut through marble. "But he . . ." "But he . . ."

Marti trails her hand along Clement's cheek and leaves him. She's already engaged with their sons. "Stop it or there's no movie tonight."

Is this it, Clement wonders. Has he given up everything he thought he was for this? No, he tells himself, because nobody is strong enough to change his life this dramatically and then say, Oops I made a mistake; D. P. Moynihan: *any institution develops an interest in its predictions and will act to protect them.* I had no choice.

Not for this. Because of that—the loneliness; he did in fact survive the seventies, along with Barty and the others, spread all over the state in parishes that never quite recovered from the holy wars. Clement kept the parish books, raised money and with all the energy left to him tried to lift diminished congregations to some sense of the eternal, wanting to share some portion of what he had felt on that long-ago night. But he was just a man and they were only people, whom he could not move with his hands or his heart or all the passion he could bring to what was after all only another human voice.

In the new drab days, Clement found himself homesick for the sumptuous liturgy that had drawn him in the first place, the implications of rapture, intimations of the absolute. The English translation was a shambles. Between the intention and the act lay a treacherous swamp of false starts and failed gestures. He couldn't even raise a decent choir.

But it wasn't that. He didn't even lose his faith. It was, by God, the loneliness; about this time one Saturday he sat in his empty church with the confessional standing open because of the heat and because penitents seldom came. He stared into the dusty shaft of light that fell in the church doors, which he had thrown wide, in hopes. Looking into the dusty light, Clement saw nothing ahead but more drab days unfolding. . . . God! In the next second he was overturned, stricken. Richard was dead and Freddy was gone and it was clear Hal was going, and Barty—he wasn't so sure about Barty—and it was not that Clement could not do what God ordained here, it was that he couldn't seem to do it very well; misery had blundered in and beggared him. He only had enough faith left for himself.

He fell in love.

They were working together in the parish CCD program; pastor and assistant, daily association sweet and stable when everything else Clement knew had shaken loose and begun to slip.

Is that it? Is that all? Did he do it because it was too hard to hang on? Lonely in his uncertainty, he fixed on Sister Martha, drew her close and clung for comfort; in time he fled his grief and lost himself in her, my love! Was there anything in earthly life that equaled that velvety slide?

At evening mass in the big old downtown church Clement puts Marti between him and the boys because he needs to concentrate. In view of everything, it's important for him to do this right. Removed from his place at the altar, where he admits his mind sometimes used to wander, Clement is passionate about the mass. This ragged feeling every time he comes in, he can't help it: *I should be up there.* Although he and Marti went through all the right channels and have been laicized, although except for the brief, duplicitous period of their courtship, Clement has kept right with the church, he feels like an outsider here. Look at him in his old black topcoat, kneeling with his family in a back pew, Clement Duval who used to be a priest. He is embarrassed.

Another thing: he is the oldest father here. There are guys here half his age with bigger families, and they don't have any trouble controlling their kids. But on the other side of Marti, Tommy squirms until she gives him a rosary to play with and three-year-old Mikey asks for it; he won't shut up. Even though Marti does a good job of keeping his whispering under control, it's like a fingernail down Clement's spine. If Mikey doesn't hush, people will begin to twist in their seats and stare, but if Clement hushes him, he may start to shriek. The priest will turn on the altar and stare at them; he loves his kids but this is impossible. He gets Marti's eye: can't she shut them up? At the sermon, which Clement attends to in spite of the fact that the priest is dull, Mikey squirms from her grip and begins crawling along the kneeler. The text is so banal Clement wishes he could get up there and. . . .

Mike! In spite of Clement's furious hiss at Marti to grab him, the child has ducked around the end of the pew and is crawling along the seat in front of them. Clement catches him in a grip so sharp that Mikey cranks up to bawl and before he can stop himself, angry, humiliated Clement grabs Marti's wrist and mutters in a stony voice, "Martha, in the name of God!" At her expression his mouth floods: *Oh Marti, please don't look like that, I take it back.* Lord, does he blame her after all?

She flushes to the eyes and picks up Mikey and her things and retreats to the soundproof room at the back of the church. Tommy, who has been self-consciously playing the good boy, takes one look at his father's face and slouches after his mother.

That's better. Yes. Embracing the silence, Clement hurls himself at the surface of the vernacular liturgy and in a feat of concentration breaks through; with all his heart he wants to be part of what's going on up there. But as the priest raises the host at the Consecration Clement's breath catches in his chest in grief for *that*. What I was.

He thinks: I can still baptize.

When he told Barty Malone he was leaving he was surprised by Barty's face; it was like the wicket in the confessional slamming shut. Of course he was going to be laicized; he ought to be grateful that change had made it a possibility. In the old days he and Sister Martha would have been condemned as adulterers and barred from the sacraments; Clement knew Barty thought he ought to be grateful for the mercy but in his deep, selfish heart Clement wanted to have both lives.

They are still friends. Barty is a monsignor now, and when he has time he comes to the Duvals' house for dinner, but he is distanced, like a landowner visiting tenant farmers, so that Clement has exchanged one loneliness for another. What ever happened to those good buddies in the hall at Montrose, those two sweet high school drunks laid out with the keg on the beach at Hull, or Saul who turned into Paul who has caused us all such grief? He loves his family but he misses the company of his own kind. What is his kind? He can't be sure, but he understands now that what he has always wanted is to have everything he has with Marti and still have this. And if he has to sacrifice one or the other?

Some days he would give anything to be up there.

He takes Communion from a man ten years his junior: "Body of Christ." The body. His. Clement's. Hers. The body of the church. God if only it is all really part of the same. He is groping toward something—can't quite make out the shape of his consolation or be certain it's there.

But the mass is over and he rejoins Marti and the children out front. It is getting dark and the premature spring warmth is gone. The light has changed so everything looks grey—the grimy face of the inner-city church, the gritty steps; even the walk where his family clumps is so bleak that the colors they are wearing stand out—bumptious Mikey and sad-looking Tom bundled in quilted jackets like egg cosies, Marti, in the red hat and scarf: that expression. Oh Marti, I'm sorry. How do people learn to make it up? *Creak.* All he can find to say to her is: "Don't be mad."

The former Sister Martha is something else now, bulky and sweet-looking in her duffle coat with those handsome kids dangling from either hand, weighing her down, and even though

Clement doesn't know how to tell his wife anything that matters, her expression makes it clear she's still his. She is pink with distress. "What do you want me to do?"

Oh Marti. Even out here in the muddy twilight his body remembers her. "It wasn't you," he says to her, understanding clearly that it was he who picked her, not the other way around; if he wasn't looking for this, then he was looking for something just like it.

Creak. He chokes on the rest: It was me. His departure from the priesthood was never her fault—or his. In ways he will never be able to spell out it was a function of his revised design. The raw and terrified Clement spread-eagled in that spare room all those years ago may have been laid open to receive precisely this.

She pushes Mikey forward, prodding "Tell Daddy," and his little boy says, "I'm sorry, Daddy," so smoothly that Clement knows he has been rehearsed.

"Oh Michael," he says, thinking, God! and the little boy clamps himself to Clement and they hug; having raged at his life and come full circle, Clement blends with his family and in the blurred passion of that instant he truly believes everything he cares about is fused or will be fused in or for eternity. Then Tommy stumbles, jarring Clement so his knee buckles and he bumps Marti so in the beginning night the family teeters on the sidewalk like a rocking toy just about to go over. "Oh Tommy," he cries, circling them with his body; Marti smiles and the best parts of himself surface and go out to meet her. He wants to give her everything. "Let's go," he says.

Queen of the Beach

My mother dresses according to her expectations.

Look at her finishing her makeup: green eye liner, with contrasting eye shadow; the tinted moisturizer matches her impressive tan, but enough is never enough for her. She's splashing blusher on her cheekbones, and lord, the shoes!

When she goes out she will be gorgeous. It's her only aim.

For the rest, Celeste is satisfied, snug in her neat beach house among her precious objects that would set your teeth on edge: shell statuary, too many Hummels, those perfumed mushroom air fresheners in the candy pastels. She has a mirrored bathroom and a Siamese cat. She does yoga, works out on her exerbikle, pedaling with the devil at her heels. With us grown and our father out of the picture, she lives a tidy life: pretty breakfasts, Lean Cuisine nuked in the microwave, old faves on the TV, everything simple, calm.

But when she shows herself to the people she is magnificent. Her taste is not my taste, but hey.

My God, the woman is in her sixties, unless she's lying and the damage is worse. She says she had me young; I know she had me late. She carries herself like a birthday present, and in certain lights you can almost see it too. She gets off on the contrast: her, me.

"Sally, that face. Why don't you smile?"

I'd rather die than tell her about me and Peter.

"The future is coming," Celeste says foolishly, as if she can hardly wait.

She is getting ready to go to the beach.

My mother has on gold neck-chains today, with gold hoops that hang almost to her shoulders; the set in her platinum hair is baked to last. I don't know whether the contrast is obscene or wonderful: wedding-cake hair, fantastic body, wrinkled face. In the bikini, she is amazing. From behind, you'd never guess.

Her stomach muscles are phenomenal. Without meaning to, she preens: *This is what exercise can do for you.* She does not see this as a holding action. Celeste still believes she can get thinner, swifter, better. Maybe she can.

Audience is everything. "What do you think?"

I am caught empty-handed. "Leopard skin."

Although she despises me for being out of shape, Celeste envies me my flesh. It is certain I will go where she is heading, but she can never come back to where I am. It is this that creates the tension between us. She thinks I am heedless of what I have been given, profligate. I think there are more important things. Later this afternoon, she'll try to make me go shopping with her and buy me something I don't want; she'll lay some bright fabric next to my face and say, "See what a little color will do for you?" She says it's important to keep your look flexible. She means I don't care how I look. The hell of it is, I do. And I look fine.

"You'd be really pretty if you'd fix yourself up."

"There's nothing the matter with me."

"Oh come on, smile. Let a little glamour into your life."

I don't want to hear this right now. "Mother."

"Please."

"Celeste."

It's a flossy name, and my mother lives up to it. Did she name me Sally to make me plain? She dressed like a star even when I was little. When she did herself up like a prom corsage and swanked into meetings at my school, I used to pretend I belonged to one of the other, ordinary women, who dressed like moms. I don't want to shrink when she makes me walk with her, but I do. We exist in mutual embarrassment; among Peter's and my friends back home, I want to put a bag over my gaudy mother's head. Today she would like to put one over mine. I am sedentary, thoughtful. At her age she still thinks of herself as a sexual object. Which of us is wrong?

"It's not who you are," she says, unfurling like a centerfold. "It's who you *think* you are that makes the difference." Today I'm particularly grateful that she spares me her usual: *If you lose your looks, you're going to lose your man and what will happen to you then?*

"Oh come on," I say. "If we're going, let's go."

She's ready; we have to get to the beach soon or she'll lose the strongest sun. She's anxious to touch up that tan but there is a problem. She's looking at my reflection in her mirror. "You're not going looking like *that.*"

Because this is the first day of the visit, I go in the bathroom and spend an extra minute with the comb. On this walk, I have to measure up. She says she'd like to show me off to her friends at the hotel, but I suspect she wants me along for contrast; I am large where she is small and neat. Probably because growing up, we fight what we know, I am aggressively natural: L. L. Bean clothes and no makeup, nothing on the hair. If I were Barbie-perfect would it reinforce her or destroy her? Although I'll never do anything about it, I feel a secret, vengeful urge to know. "Better?"

"Better. We all have to make the most of what we've got."

I know what is expected. "Not everybody was born with your looks."

"Ah." Because this is only the first day and she is hopeful, she says, "It's wonderful having you here. I wish you could stay forever."

I strangle. "Mmm." I am here to . . . I don't know why I am here, but she is my mother, I have to do this, and every time we meet hope rises up like the phoenix bird. She hopes I will be more the daughter she wants and I hope things will be different.

"I can make you a place on the sun porch." Lovingly, she pats the air.

"I'd love to," I say, "but I have a family." This is only partly a lie.

"I'm just so happy you are here." She really wants to be.

In fact, my mother and I can only take each other in limited doses. Celeste forgets; we are too close, too disparate to sit comfortably together. There's a whirring in the air between us: the buzz and clatter of souls at cross-purposes. When we meet we fuse, locked in the terrible ancient pattern, mother and daughter, gog and magog, yang and yin, or is it Chang and Eng?

"You could go walking with me every day." She's half afraid I may take her up on this.

"I would only cramp your style."

"It would do you good," she says with a worried look. She thinks I'm in terrible shape. I can't for the life of me say whether she wants me to shape up for my sake or hers. Dissatisfied with me, she turns and picks up something from her dressing table. She feints. "Here."

Instinctively, I flinch.

"Then put it on yourself," she says.

The lipstick is worn to a strange-looking point, it has mother-germs on it. I'm only here for three days. I can stand on my head for three days. I put on Celeste's lipstick and we go out.

She hasn't the faintest idea how much this costs me, any more than she knows what else I have on my mind right now, because beyond the most perfunctory "How are you," Celeste doesn't really want to know. Even when I lived at home my mother never asked how things were with me in the deep part, where I live. I'd rather die than tell her, then or now. My gaudy little mother pulls me out of the house, rattling on like a girl. As we head for the beach she says, "There's a Clinique special at Maas Brothers. I'll get you color-analyzed. My treat."

Oh mother. Oh captor. Thanks.

Every day she walks five miles on the beach. She likes to start at the public beach and walk north, past private houses, past the conventioneers and chic Europeans sunning in front of the Don

Ce-sar. At a distance, she still turns heads: the neat figure, the jewelry, the astounding pile of hair. She can't help judging women's bodies: *young but flabby*, or: *scrawny*, or, with satisfaction: *fat*. Sometimes she's shocked: "Look, a nice old lady just about my age. She doesn't have to let herself go like that." Judgment reinforces her. My life is worth the effort. See?

She usually finishes at the Hilton, where she likes to rent one of the hooded chaises and sit for a while, with those pearly nails clicking on her glass—a little something from the bar. Sometimes she has lunch there; sometimes she meets a man; at her age she is so graceful with them that I wonder what's wrong with me. I am klunky, whereas she . . . the woman is twice my age and yet shimmering just beneath the surface I see the successful high school flirt. Celeste will stay long enough to get her money's worth out of today's costume and when she's good and ready she'll start back.

The exercise keeps her in wonderful shape. On these ceremonial visits, Celeste's forced marches leave me gasping, while she trots along, jabbering heedlessly. For all she cares, I could be anyone. But she is my mother and I have to do this, at least this once.

At the municipal beach we stop under the palm frond shelter while she shucks the coverup and oils herself like a walnut chair. Except where fugitive pigment has mottled her legs and arms with white, Celeste has a furniture-polish tan. She proffers the oil; I refuse.

"You need to be careful, Sally," she says. "You know this Florida sun."

I shrug. "I'll keep my shirt on."

"You'll be hot." Her look says: maybe better. Let the people wonder what Sally's body is doing underneath.

I also keep my shoes on, although Celeste points out that walking in the sand smooths jagged skin off the heels. She has iridescent spots on her toes—nails like cultured pearls.

"Don't you ever think about anything but your body?"

"My clothes," she says without turning a spray-coated hair. "It's important to pay attention to your clothes."

It's important to me to keep my head down, as if we are not related. She is the exotic and I am the—am just plain Sally going along, waiting for it to be afternoon and us to be coming back.

"Cheer up and when we get to the Hilton I'll buy you lunch."

How can she know I can hardly stand to watch her eat?

"Oh, Sally. Look at the sky!"

I look up and trip on an uneven place in the sand.

In the absence of conversation, she begins. "Your father was a really thoughtful man—earrings, new blouses; he let me know he cared how I looked."

There is a silence. She is waiting for me to say something about me and Peter, the next move in the old game. Instead I counter with a question. "Then why did you cut him off?"

"Oh," she says smoothly, "we all need to be happy. It was something I had to do, and your father. . . . All your father wants to do now is get old."

"Is that so bad?"

"It may be good enough for him," she says, "but it isn't good enough for me."

I am preoccupied, but I'm still mad at her about the lipstick. "It's not his fault he's getting old," I say. I think: How could you leave him, when he loved you? It is as if she hears.

Her voice is sharp. "Don't presume."

"It seems like a pretty superficial. . . ."

She cuts me off. "I needed to be happy. I." She falters. "You can't let unhappy people drag you down with them, you have to keep it—upbeat." She is trotting so fast that I can barely catch what's coming out of her mouth, much less credit it. "Your life. . . . You reach the point. . . . You either go forward or give up."

"Mother!"

She pretends not to hear. Her bracelets rattle down her arm as she waves. "Look at that woman. Not even forty, and look at that belly. The saddlebags."

"She looks all right to me."

"That's your problem," she says; she too is angry. "Understand, you have to be careful. Vigilant. You have to watch out for the signs." Lord, what does she think she. . . . What is she trying to tell me? "You can't afford to let anything go by. Not even the smallest thing. Or else you end up. . . ." She won't finish.

I keep my head down so she can't see my face. "Look," I say foolishly, trying to distract her, "that's a really skinny one."

"You can't be too skinny," she snaps.

I strike out, forging past her and to her frustration, staying three or four paces ahead. I don't want her to see how angry I really am. This is not because I'm trying to spare her feelings, but because she would take it as a five-point addition to her score. Soon enough I'm out of breath and I have to drop back.

"Your father was always very tender with me," she says in a light voice. It's as if nothing has happened between us. "He always kissed me with his mouth open just the slightest bit, and he never forced anything—oh!"

As I watch, her knee buckles and she almost falls. Some strange need to see how she handles this keeps me from reaching out. As I suspected, Celeste manages to catch her balance and right herself; her lips are shaking, and underneath the brilliant hair I think I see the shape of the skull. I am her daughter; what's my responsibility here? A beat too late, I say, "What's the matter?"

She looks down. "It's nothing."

I can see it, smearing her foot underneath caked sand. "You're bleeding!"

She considers the insult. "Glass." Standing on one leg, she pulls it out.

We are stuck halfway between the Don and the Hilton. In transatlantic air flights or cheap airplane movies, this would be called the point of no return. My heart leaps up; I see escape.

"Let's go up to Gulf Boulevard. Take my arm. Listen, I'll treat you to a cab."

Celeste looks at me in such chagrin that I wonder if there's something she isn't telling me. "But my new bathing suit. The Hilton." In the classic posture of the mother buying favors, she says cleverly, "I was going to treat you to lunch."

"It's OK, really." I am like a prisoner of war with the end of the march in sight, wondering whether this is really the end and I'm going to be all right or if there are worse tortures ahead. "There's always tomorrow."

Her look says: No there isn't. She lifts her head so the hoop earrings flip and glitter. "No. Really, I'm fine."

"Your foot is bleeding." All I want to do is get out of the sun.

"The Hilton. It's Thursday. Miles and Barry will be there."

"Barry?"

"No one you know." My God, the woman is twice my age, she's hurt herself, but she looks at me over her shoulder like a forties movie star. She shakes me off. She favors the foot for a second; then she shrugs and sets it down hard. She's off. "The Hilton has a buffet on Thursdays. We're practically there."

It's twenty minutes away, but Celeste doesn't want to hear that from me. I have to fall in behind her, wondering whether, like Oscar Wilde's little mermaid, she will leave footprints filled with blood.

"It isn't that bad," she says, trotting on a diagonal. "Here. The water will wash it out."

In a way I am relieved; she's fine. It occurs to me that sooner or later I really am going to have to take care of this woman, but not yet, not yet. It is remarkable to be going along behind Celeste, watching her switching shoulders and the firm butt moving under the leopard-printed Orlon suit which I understand, suddenly, lets in the sunlight for that all-over tan. Yes she is proud.

Now I want you to regard her—you, who are not a member of our family, don't know her, don't know me. Take in her total look: the suit, the nails, that walk. Her age. Is there a time to turn all that off—the profusion of expectations? What do we have here, is it an obscenity or is it gallantry?

But we are arriving at the hotel. Yes Miles is here and Barry is here, two nice old guys in boxer suits with baggy bellies and touchingly raffish grins who greet us with a warmth that makes everything worth it all over again for Celeste.

I am embarrassed by the smile she turns on me, pushing me forward like a kid at a recital. "My daughter." She shines.

Miles shakes my hand. "I would have known you anywhere."

"Why you're the image of your mother," sweet old Barry says. Abashed, I duck my head like a little girl and she bridles. In no way are we the same person. "Celeste, what's happened to your foot?"

When they see the cut they make a fuss, order vodka, send cabana boys for antiseptic and bandages while my mother lets herself sink gracefully into their care and I stand by like the wallflower at the ninth grade dance, trying to decide whether it's offensive or sweet—this act that they are all engaged in, courting, or is it pretending, youth: lord, their expressions. Strip away the aging surface and you can see the kids they think they are. It takes a while for the cut to stop bleeding and even longer for the trembly gents to wash out the sand that's been ground into her cut by the long walk to the hotel.

When lunch is finally over, my heart leaps up. Celeste is definitely lame. Maybe one of these sweet old men has a car. If not, I can certainly force her into a cab.

She stands. "Well boys."

"Mother," I say under my breath, "with your foot. . . ."

She hurls a look that cuts my skull in two. She comes here on her own feet every day. She will make it back. She tells Miles and Barry goodbye as if she's leaving the prom. As we head toward the beach she doesn't even limp.

The next hour is terrible. Pain makes my mother's teeth clash; the skin around her eyes and mouth is turning white. Celeste walks gingerly, but keeps her pace even and her back straight. More than once I reach out to support her; angrily she shakes me off. "Not here."

"Just let me. . . ."

"Sally, don't do that."

"Come *on*."

"Sally, I won't." Finally she hisses at me, "Goddammit, stop. I will. Not. Let them. See me like that." If I touch her again, she's going to lose control and break the mother's first commandment. If I don't stop helping, Celeste will hit me in the face.

The light has shifted. We are approaching the end point. "Well," she says, "we made it."

"But we didn't have to."

She turns on me, saying grimly, "Don't you tell me what we do and don't have to do." Limping up the municipal beach to the shelter where she's left her things, Celeste, my mother, completes the thought. She is my captain, laying out the line of march. "If you don't learn anything else from me, Sally, learn this."

Drawing herself up, she creates a hush into which she lets the next words fall. "No matter what happens to you, *you can't afford to let it show.*"

Now I am listening hard. I have told her nothing about the misery with Peter. Does she know what's happening with us in spite of my best efforts to dissemble? What my mother says next makes it clear that although she will never reproach me with it, she understands everything.

Intent, careless of our family's past, she finishes, casting a refracting light on their lives together, on everything I think I know. "Listen. The worse things are, the better you have to look."

My childhood—those costumes; I ask the question she will never answer. "You mean, all that time with Daddy, you were. . . ."

She astounds me with love: "Oh my darling," she says, "it's not what happens to you that makes the difference. It's the way you handle it."

I am surprised by what I feel. "Oh, Mom!" I have my hands out; I'm waiting for her to reorder my life for me and set it back down in them. "What else. What else?"

But Celeste has given all she has to give. Now she's cleaning the sand off her feet, off the bandage, which has peeled away to reveal the angry cut. "That's all," she says. "That's all you have to know." She backs off because I am standing too close.

When I look into her face like this, I suppose I ought to see my own death forecast exactly, but that would be a cliche. When my mother lifts her shoulder and tosses her pretty earrings like that I see instead the persistence of faith. My God, she thinks she can go on like this forever.

"After I change, we're going shopping."

"Shopping." Some day, too soon, I will hold her leached head in my two hands and see her to the door she is approaching, but I understand what we are trying to do here. "Of course." We will.

Thing of Snow

I go funny in winter, Martin says, spreading his fingers because he can never explain it—he gets strange in spite of the fixed and soothing manifestations of the deepest part of the year.

Between winters he forgets, so that each year his slow, silent descent comes as a surprise. Encased in solitude, he presses his forehead against the cold glass of his bedroom window, straining to see into the early dark, the fresh, incessant snow. He makes up excuses for not going out and in time descends into deep winter, calling in sick and sending out for food so he can dream on and on in dry, overheated rooms.

Then one day he is arrested by a dark shape: the bare window, the blackness outside; at first the glass gives back only his reflection, but then at its back Martin sees a blurred shape moving, his bad old trouble, the fear. Oh! Leaning closer, he can see through his reflection to the snow outside, the night, and with a suddenness that always surprises him, suffers the complete return of the winter he spent at Edgemont. With the process completed, he's relieved; the weirdness, the muffled, seductive winter dreams are his souvenir of that particular time.

I go funny in winter, he tells people, almost complacent in the fond, full knowledge of what's happening.

Immured in his bright apartment he can taste the snow of that winter and feel it on his face; it stays with him even as he sees without wanting to that last sharp vision of his friend Trot, the accusation in her face. *I go funny in winter;* there are still times when he's afraid he will have to rush outside and hurl himself in the snow; will have to burrow until he is one with it, covered by the voluptuous, unending fall.

They all lived together at Edgemont in that last winter of his madness, Martin and Howie and Desmond and Trot. They lived with other patients in a dark Victorian heap where brown window frames rose from the floor to a point almost out of sight and frosted glass fixtures hung from remote, shadowy ceilings painted an institutional cream. It was a steam-heated winter; they could see their breath on the windows and by February their skin had dried and their hair was lifeless. Talking to his psychiatrist, Martin would scratch endlessly, unable to stop brittle nails from raking his flaking skin.

They were all getting better; the doctors said so. That's why they were in this halfway house. In buildings higher up the hill sad wraiths clung to metal-grilled windows; from time to time the lights flickered, and Martin and the others winced as at some distant electrocution. If they pressed him the attendant would mumble something about the generator but remembering shock treatments, Martin and the others knew what drained the rooms of light. Joking, they threatened each other: I'll have you sent back up the hill.

Even so, Martin remembered his time at Edgemont as one of perfect safety. There was a doctor to talk to when the fears began to bloat and close his throat so he couldn't breathe; there were drugs, there was help even when it wasn't needed and Martin could tell himself there was somebody in charge. He needed to know this; it was a manifestation of his particular illness, for at its worst fear disabled him and he needed help to talk and eat, to keep on breathing in and out. They'd found him paralyzed in his room at college one September, waiting for help to come, and they had brought him here.

Now he was getting better; they all were, and still he and lovely, gaunt Trot and the others clung to the walls like sick plants, languishing without purpose and spinning out old fears to fill the hours.

The young men were of an age—Martin; elegant Desmond, the failed actor; Howie, with the powerful shoulders and the neanderthal slouch, who had cracked in his first year of graduate school, running a fist through the window on every landing in the HGS. Feverish Trot was no age; she was everything or nothing, would not talk about herself. She played at being friends with passion, learning all their passwords, inventing new games to amuse them and listening as they repeated themselves endlessly and without boredom. They played bridge and made up endless word games, smoking stale cigarettes and looking for their own warped reflections in the black formica tabletop. Playing Crash, they made up extravagant combinations, vying for Trot.

"Who would you save in a head-on car crash?" Howie said, "Dinah Washington or George Washington?"

Desmond passed it off with an actorish wave. "Would you save Saint or Boy George?"

Martin fell into it from habit; he used to make up parallels in bed and save them for the next round. "Saint or Key Luke?"

"No," Howie growled. "Dinah or George Washington. You have to make up your mind."

Trot said quietly, "Dinah's only a woman."

Desmond snorted. "But George had false teeth."

"Ghengis or Aly Khan?" Martin had been saving it.

Howie scowled blackly. "The Washingtons. You have to decide."

Desmond got up so fast his chair scraped. "I don't want to make up my mind. I just want to get out of here."

"I want to go home," Trot said. "Do you think they'll ever let me go back to my life?"

"Sure they will," Martin said firmly. *As soon as you stop trying to hurt yourself.* Grinned like a car salesman. "We're all getting better. That's why they put us here."

Trot grimaced. "Lucky us."

"Dinah or George Washington," Howie said.

Desmond spun and bolted. "Shut up, Howie. We have to get out of here."

It was almost dark; the snow was falling relentlessly and Martin wanted to stay warm and watch it from the window; he would just sit at this table and pretty soon the bell would ring and dinner would come. But the others were leaving; they were waiting for him; Trot pulled his hand. "Come on, Martin."

"It's too cold."

"Never mind." Desmond was in the doorway, inflating with restlessness. "Meet you in five minutes. Wear boots."

"You think you're so damn smart," Howie said because he resented Desmond's speed and grace, "you and your damn excursions. You're just afraid to sit here and decide." But even he had lost interest; he stood flexed, the broad jumper sizing up the gorge. "Martin?"

At other tables people were watching him, muttering and twittering; the attendant was watching too, and because the four did everything together, because he had to spite or deny all onlookers Martin fell in behind Howie, saying, too loud, "We're out of here."

At the last minute he faltered; looking into the snow and darkness of the late afternoon he hung back, but Howie stumped downstairs in a red and black lumber jacket and outside, Desmond beckoned. Trot fidgeted at his elbow, the cliche snow maiden with high boots and a fur hat pulled down over her bright curls. They were all cliche figures that day: Desmond slender and darkly handsome; heavyset Howie clomping along in galoshes with flapping metal clasps; impatient, dancing Trot— and Martin, the pale and indecisive wraith. They were cliches; it wasn't any of it real and so Martin was able to follow the others into the darkness, looking back at the watching attendant to say, as if creating a talisman: "We'll be back."

The attendant nodded. "I know you will."

Outside the flakes hung in clumps, hitting them without force, and when he looked up Martin saw the sky was still light, enclosing them; it was like being inside a paperweight.

Howie bunched some snow in his hand. "It's going to lay."

108 / KIT REED

Desmond turned that actor's profile. "It's one hell of a snow."

"We ought to do something about it."

Trot threw the first snowball. "It's beautiful."

"Let's *do* something." It was choking him. Dizzy, he swelled and let out all his breath in a yell. "Let's make something. Let's make some hell of a thing."

Desmond was darting, promoting a snow fight.

"Hell with snow fights," Martin said. In charge; he was in charge!

"We could go traying," Howie said. "Look at that hill!"

"No, we have to make something." Martin saw his friends dipping and turning like wild birds; in a minute they would spin out of control. He was aware not so much of the outlines as the mass of the buildings on the hill above him and he said, urgently, "Let's make something that'll scare the socks off the crazies up there."

"A dragon," Desmond said, catching fire.

Howie sketched with his hands. "Lots of teeth."

Trot laughed. "George Washington."

"No." Martin turned now; he had them. "A dinosaur."

Trot whirled, delighted. "A dinosaur!"

And so, looking back, Martin would see that it had been his idea from the beginning; the whole thing had been his fault after all. The friends fell on their knees, packing snow, but the faster they worked the faster the wind displaced it and they fell back, finally.

"It isn't laying," Howie said in disgust.

"Tomorrow then," Martin said doggedly. "Tomorrow it's going to freeze."

Desmond sat back on his haunches. "Can't. I have a date."

Martin barked, "Tell her another time."

Trot ran a snow-clotted mitten across Desmond's cheek. "Baby, you always have me."

Curving automatically to hug her, Desmond looked over Trot's shoulder at Martin. It might still have gone the other way but Martin was casting about him; he caught a flicker in the dark and the snow seemed to part so it came clear: the ugly lighted windows on the hill. "We have to show the bastards," he said, not sure what he meant.

Desmond fell into Martin's hands. "Scare the hell out of them."

And so they were going to do it after all.

Trot came for him too early the next morning; women weren't even allowed on that floor, but when he woke she was in his room. "Come on," she hissed. "We're going to need a lot of stuff."

For the moment Martin was content to watch her from the warmth of his bed. Her face was a bright, febrile pink under the wool hat and he remembered hearing something about TB patients and he wondered if all sanitaria were the same; he might have tried to pull her down with him but his illness had made him timid and now she was yanking clothes off a hook, throwing them at him.

"Dress," she said. "I'm getting the sandwiches."

He stayed inside the covers a minute longer watching the light swim on the ceiling, and as he lay there he was filled, almost overcome, by a blinding feeling of potential, of eager joy so intense that it frightened him and he had to get up quickly before it consumed him. He dressed and went downstairs in a rush, pulling his elation around him like some exotic, shining cloak. The others were just as excited; trembling with haste, they wolfed coffee and rolls in the empty dining room and then, before anybody in the house woke, they went out into the snow.

Their equipment was elaborate. They had shovels and carving tools and water to freeze the superstructure and a wheelbarrow to bring snow; they had sandwiches and coffee and Howie had brought dry wood for a fire. Desmond was busy on the back of an envelope, sketching as he walked; Trot had a tape measure coiled around her neck. Martin's boots were heavy and he stepped out in an unconscious swagger. He was sure people were watching from the house. He dragged his scarf from his neck and waved it like a banner, thinking: you poor sods.

The sunlight on the snow dizzied him, leaving afterimages, and so Martin was never sure whether there really were strange, sad people watching from grilled windows on the hill; if there

were, then it only underscored his own happiness and freedom. He was filled, elevated, somehow *more* than he had been
before he got sick and they brought him here. The sky was brilliant and every outline was distinct, beautiful and intense; seeing, Martin wanted to arrest life at that moment, fixing the
images like gems inside a crystal globe.

Desmond may have sensed it too, perhaps seeing at the same
time the logical end to such follies; his laughter was sharp as he
turned suddenly, assuming the weight of the whole enterprise:
"Here," he said. "We'll build it here."

They worked for hours, wearing paths with the wheelbarrow,
shaping and packing and pouring water on the body of their
dinosaur and waiting for it to freeze. They worked with such
concentration that they had no idea what time it was; at ten they
solemnly devoured the sandwiches, fully convinced that it was
time for lunch. Then the sun soared higher and they were hun-
gry again. This time it was noon and, grudgingly, they went
back to the house to eat.

Martin thought he'd stifle before they were free again. The
dry air of the house clamped him tight and he was oppressed by
the other patients, who fluttered in the dining room like dying
leaves. They took a corner table and Howie forced the window,
throwing it wide while other patients frowned and shivered
elaborately. Their own faces were bright with well-being and
they laughed more than they needed to. Martin was already
wild to get away; still Howie sat across from him, chewing relentlessly, and Desmond held Trot's hand, spinning a story about
a snow cavern and the thwarted lover who buried his girl alive
so that the villagers came the next morning to find her enshrined,
an ice princess with outstretched arms.

"You can see her in the Louvre."

Stifling, Martin pushed back his chair. "Let's get out of here."

Graceful Desmond lounged. "What's your hurry?"

"We have to finish." One more minute and he. . . .

Slouching, Desmond yawned. "We don't *have* to do anything."

Trot had mercy. "Come on." She ran a hand down Desmond's cheek. "We'll build your snow cavern next."

When they got back to the mound of snow they'd been working on all morning they were surprised to see how small it was.

"You on the tail brigade," Desmond said, "You're slow, slow, slow."

Howie hugged Trot. "We're trying to relate."

"He won't identify with me."

"You have to verbalize your problems," Martin said automatically.

Desmond placed a heap of snowballs by the dinosaur's tail: droppings. "Psychiatry."

Howie still had Trot by the shoulder; Martin wanted to pry his fingers loose. "I'm here for her."

She slipped from under his arm. "I'm developing healthy attitudes."

"Come on," Martin said, not sure why this made him angry. "It's late."

Howie began kicking snow. "Let's turn this thing into a fort."

"We could go to town for coffee," Desmond said.

Angry Howie said, "Not all of us."

Martin reminded him, "You and Trot are the only ones with passes."

Swift Desmond grinned. "I know."

Howie kicked the dinosaur. "Let's smash this thing."

"No!"

"We could turn it into a naked lady."

"Stop that! They're watching!" Martin backed into the snow figure, standing with his arms spread protectively. "They're waiting for us to fuck up." Howie scowled and the other two stood at a little distance, holding hands; if he didn't think fast he would lose these people; he had to keep them working, make them work through dinner if that's what it took, stopping only to warm their hands at the fire; they had to keep at this until they had patted the final gob of snow into place. "Let's show them," he began, not sure whether he meant the doctors or someone else; he had a vision of the crazies in the K ward. Leaping and gulping air, they would wake to find a giant dinosaur rushing at them from below. "We have to *show* the bastards."

"You're getting compulsive."

"No. Let's show them where it is." He swung his arms, taking in the halfway house, the hill, inflated, let it all out in a roar. "It's out here."

He fell to without even looking to see whether they were with him, so absorbed that he wasn't sure who first moved in next to him, packing snow with firm, almost vindictive strokes. Desmond's voice trailed past him like a banner:

"For England, Harry and Saint George."

Then Howie began singing, whumping on each downbeat as he pounded on more snow. Trot was beside Martin now, working with quick, purposeful hands, and he had for the moment an eerie sense of joint or communal existence; the four of them were a gestalt, a small, ferocious machine built for this single act of creation, and the idea made him shout. It didn't interrupt anything; it didn't signify because his sound was their sound now; it was not his animal but their animal, and they worked without a break until Martin fell back finally, all at once cold and depleted because they were almost done. The sky had gone pink and grey while they weren't looking; the afternoon was on the wane.

With an effort he bent to the project again, dribbling watery snow to give the dinosaur an expression. He stopped to smooth the creature's flank and was aware of Trot's hand under his, discovering at the same time that his hand was so numb he could hardly feel the shape of hers. The chill was on him and above the light was going, and in his regret, in an almost despairing wish to forestall the night he took off his glove, warming his hand in the incredible curve of her neck. In the next second Trot was leaning into him and he had both hands inside her collar now, murmuring senselessly at the soft flesh, and he might have pulled her away—into the snow? Into the house? He would never know because there was Howie hovering over him, smoldering. In the next second he had yanked Trot away, saying: "Leave her alone."

She tugged until Howie let go and then she stood at a little distance saying almost apologetically: "I'd better get some more stuff for the fire."

Martin was saying to Howie, "I'll do what I bloody want to."

"She's not yours."

"She's not anybody's." Desmond was leaning against the flank of the dinosaur, smooth and snide.

"We'd better get the hell finished." Martin looked over his shoulder, pressed by time.

Desmond was laughing—at him? "I'll go help with the fire."

As the light went the fire seemed to grow, twisting their shadows and altering the dinosaur's outlines with every flicker. Howie and Martin worked with absorption, falling back finally to discover that they were working alone. At some distance there was the fire and beyond that they could see the shapes of Desmond and Trot, close, merging; it may only have been the warp of the flames but Martin thought he saw them sinking, settling back on a bed of snow. He never knew for sure because Howie was already plunging toward them, crying, "Dammit, goddammit," and then he heard his own high, inadvertent voice:

"We have to finish, we have to *finish*." He could hear himself pleading, "Come on, come *on*."

Howie was standing over them with his mittened fists floating, angry and aimless, while Trot struggled to her feet with a little murmur of distress, saying, "Come on Howie, let's go help Martin finish."

But Desmond still had her hand, trying to pull her down, and Howie made an angry lunge. "Dammit!"

Laughing, Desmond rolled away.

"Come on," Trot said, distraught. "Oh Howie, come *on*."

They were all miserable; their clothes had been wet through for some hours and with the sun gone, their mittens and sleeves had begun to freeze. Martin could feel an icy strip where his gloves fell short, and the cold crept through all the layers he had put on to protect himself. In a while his joints would solidify; they would find him in the morning, the fallen sculptor frozen to his work. They were all miserable and now they were working feverishly, revolving and colliding aimlessly, like billiard balls after the split. On his way back from the fire he bumped into Trot and dropped the pan of water he was carrying, splashing them both; he thought he felt the water burning his skin, hers. She leaned into him and he could feel her shivering.

"Martin, I'm so tired."

The water in their clothes was freezing, bonding her skin and his. "We're almost finished, Trot, we'll just finish and then, and then. . . ."

Trembling, she said fiercely, "I just want to get warm."

His numb hands traveled over her, discovering nothing but the bulky outlines of her clothes; even so his brain was afire and he heard himself murmuring, "We'll finish and then you'll be warm, we'll be warm, we'll be everything we can. . . ." Martin was aware of her voice coming and going under his own and he would never know whether she had been saying yes yes yes at that moment or protesting, pulling him closer and saying, over and over, no no no.

"You son of a bitch."

Howie spoke from nowhere, spinning Martin around and throwing him down in the snow. Martin could hear Trot crying out and imagined that they had been frozen together like a tongue to an ice tray; the ice bonding them ripped now, tearing skin. Then Howie fell on him and there was nothing but cold and blindness and hard blows so muffled by all the clothes they were wearing that Martin, at least, could not feel any of them. They grappled and rolled, growling, arrested by a pure, clear note: Trot's voice, going up and up.

When they stood she was crying, "Stop it," sobbing into Desmond's front. He had an arm around her and he was murmuring into her hair, "It's all right, it's all right."

Desmond tightened his arms, hugging Trot and laughing when Howie lowered his head and tried to charge him, stumbling in the rutted snow. Passionate Howie said, "It's not fair, it's just not fair," but his body betrayed him, so that his feet got tangled in snow.

"Fair's fair," Desmond said, but Trot broke away from him.

"Stop it," she said, crying hard, "if you guys would only *stop.*"

Martin went toward her, wanting to make her feel better, but she jumped away. "I know what," Trot said desperately; she was reaching, trying to create something with her hands.

Desmond crooned, "What, baby?"

"Let's build your snow cavern." Her voice was too bright.

Howie frowned. "Snow cavern?"

"You know—the ice princess." She forced a smile.

"That crap."

She ran off a little distance, drawing them along. "We could make me into a snow statue. Come on."

Martin said hopelessly, "But we haven't finished. . . ."

"First we can make the cavern." Trot was improvising, building on air.

"I know where there's a ready-made cavern," Desmond said.

They took torches, following him to a stand of blue spruce halfway up the hill. Two of the trees had been stripped partway up the trunk and the branches formed an arc taller than their heads, the whole muffled and glittering with snow; the hill slanted down and away so that it was like stepping into a small, arched shrine where no winds blew. Trot whispered, "It's wonderful."

It was. And she? What was the matter with her? "Here," she said urgently, "First you have to make my throne."

They set torches in the snow and worked without saying anything, not sure why they were doing what she told them or what would happen when they finished, but when they had shaped a small mound they looked around for Trot and saw that she was standing at a little distance, already unwinding her scarf and unzipping her jacket, working at the buttons of her sweater and yanking at the undershirt.

"Here," Desmond said with exquisite smoothness, "I'll help you."

"You can make a mold on me," Trot said. "It's going to be beautiful."

She took off her bra and Martin was so mesmerized by the shadows, the light on her body, that he stood for a second and let it happen, watching as Trot sat down on the snow and waited for them to begin packing snow around her feet. He saw that she would sit there until she froze if she had to, immuring or immolating herself to quiet them, serene and suicidal in her icy retreat; he saw too that in another minute he was going to join them, packing snow on a body already grown cold, burying with it his own pains and doubts, sealing them under a glassy layer of snow. He stood where he was, wavering; he might have frozen there but he felt a *ting*, a tiny explosion in his skull, the aura of something returning, and in the next second recognized the fear that had brought him here in the first place. Then, terrified because he had to escape it, he pushed the other two out of the way and yanked at Trot, yelling:

"Stop! You're all crazy!"

It was easy to push Howie and Desmond aside but it was hard to get freezing Trot to her feet, mortally hard to bring her back to life. He managed to get the skirt and jacket on her and then he and the others dragged, pushed and carried her back to the building, hauling her over the snow. Desmond and Howie might have taken her to her room and put her in bed and left her there shuddering, would have fled and lay low in the coffee shop until she died or got better, but intent, angry Martin could not quit with this, perhaps because it was in part his fault.

He put her down on her bed. Grimly, he stood watch.

She was a strange color now, but her eyes burned and her teeth clashed. "So thank you," she said hurriedly, "now 'bye."

Martin set his jaw. "We have to call somebody."

Shuddering, Trot said, "No." She swung her wet head from side to side on the pillow, pleading. "Please no."

"You'll get pneumonia."

"Then let me."

"You'll die." Martin turned abruptly. "I'm getting the doctor."

"Please, please don't. Just leave me alone." She was tossing on the bed; in a minute the jacket would part and he would be able to look at her again; it might be what she wanted; the wool fell away and underneath she was beautiful, crying, "Please don't do this to me."

"Trot, I have to." Still he lingered by the bed, considering.

She tried to get up. "They'll send me back up the hill."

Desmond and Howie hung in the doorway like shadows: who, us? We're clean. Desmond said, "Come on, man, you wouldn't do that to her."

"Please don't," she said wildly. "Martin, I'm in love with you."

And in the next second he surprised them both. "You're lying."

Martin turned to the others with an air of discovery. "Hey, she's lying." But they were gone. He felt her hand; she was trying to pull him down, to head off what they both knew was coming, but he freed himself and with a great sense of clarity, of growing responsibility, he said, "It's going to be all right, Trot. It might even be better," and then left the room quickly, so he wouldn't have to see her face. Outside he was almost halted in his tracks by a fierce, tangible wave of pain and although he would press himself against winter windows for the rest of his life, straining into the darkness trying to make it out, he would never see it clear. He would never know whether the pain was at his own rebirth, or for something he would try to plumb in every winter that followed, a small but irrevocable loss.

—For Butch Masterson

Mr. Rabbit

Yay, hooray, we're going to see Mr. Rabbit." The children were bounding ahead of her, almost lost in the deep grass.

"Mr. *Abbott,* boys." Nan raised her voice, bringing them back to her side. "His name is Mr. Abbott."

Tad said, "Is it nice at Mr. Rabbit's house?"

"I'm sure it is, but if you call him Mr. Rabbit I'm going to kill you."

Jake giggled. "Mr. Rabbit, Mr. Rabbit."

"Mr. Rabbit," Nan said, in spite of herself. "He lives at the top of the hill with James." It sounded like something out of a children's book and it fit today; it fit with the perfect sky and the flower-studded fields. She had bought the country for the summer, and the air was full of promise and the hillside so bright that she was sure nothing bad could ever happen here; she could walk alone at night in voluptuous safety and a child could start at the top of a hill and roll over and over all the way to the bottom without hitting a single sharp stick or jagged stone.

Jake was saying, "Party, Mommy, party."

"Well I don't know how much of a party it's going to be." He and Tad weren't listening but she went on anyway. "Just us and a few of his special friends. Edward Claren and his mother, and maybe Miss Brill."

Tad said, "I hope it's a big party."

"Well at least we're invited somewhere," she said, and heard her own voice lift.

The children ran ahead, more excited than they ought to be, already expecting too much. The grass was moving in the light breeze, lifting and parting almost before the boys trampled it, making a path to the house at the top of the hill. She heard their voices rising, they had gone beyond words to pure sound, and she knew she ought to quiet them but she was excited too; they were going to a party in a new place, where nobody knew them, which meant there would be no sympathetic murmurs as they came in, and if they laughed too much there would be nobody to point out how brave they were, or how frivolous. Going into Mr. Rabbit's house, they could be brand new.

Widowed, Nan couldn't remember when she'd last been invited anywhere for her own sake and not just because somebody had decided to be nice. After she lost her true and only husband, all her friends had applied charity like Band-Aids, sneaking sidelong looks to see whether she'd recovered enough so they could quit. In recent months they had begun to look at her in some surprise: What, you still around? They had all expected her to change in some respect, to remarry or to move away, or if she remained, to be augmented: take a lover, take night classes, anything, because bereft as she was, she was not *enough*. As long as she came to their parties as she was, with no new defenses, it didn't matter how intelligent she was, or how pretty, they all withdrew as if she cried out her need with every word she spoke, as if she had loss written on her face. Coming in to a cocktail party, she wanted to approach the women with her hands outspread, saying, Look, I'm clean; I don't want to take your husbands, all I want is to have a good time. They may even have understood that, but they withdrew because they saw in Nan not so much a threat as the embodiment of their own fears, the image of losses yet to come. Uneasy with her, the men seemed to see mirrored in her their own mortality, and even in their generosity, those occasional spurts of gallantry, she could sense their reserve. They said, You can count on me any time; but they meant, Don't ask anything of me.

In the beginning her friends had besieged her with calls and invitations, but the calls tapered off because for them charity was feasible only so long as they thought of it as an intermediary step, a temporary tiding over until the object of it all began a new life, or moved away, or changed. They had to see it as something finite; at the end they wanted to be able to congratulate themselves, saying, Look what we've done.

She was free of them now. When she came in to Mr. Rabbit's party she would not have to see her own past history, like an extra person in the room. She was new in this summer town, and the first time she met Mr. Rabbit at a cocktail party she hadn't had to be a widow; she could be frivolous and entertaining, a pretty girl at a party—no more, no less. He had asked her about her hotel, nodding when she told him about the dreary progression of couples to the dining room: young, middle-aged, old. She had not added: corporations, closed. She remembered his saying, almost as if offering an expedient: "Well, my dear, not everyone wants to go two by two."

Now she was invited to dinner. She had offered to get a babysitter but he had pressed her to bring the boys, saying he loved children, he would have something special for them to eat and she could put them to bed in his room. It had crossed her mind that she might be better off leaving them but she thought: Why should they have to stay home with their old selves when I'm going someplace new? They were so happy now that she was glad she'd brought them.

"I hope he has candy." Tad had doubled back to take her hand.

"Ginger ale, more likely," she said. Then she went on because it was the first time in too long she had found anything good to tell him. "But Mr. Rabbit has a dog and he likes to cook. And I bet there'll be something special for dessert."

This is how Jake betrayed his father: "And maybe some day he'll be our daddy?"

Although she had not met James, she said with some certainty, "I don't think he's going to be anybody's daddy, dear."

The house looked like it had been painted just this summer; there were geraniums in the window boxes and flowering trees set in concrete urns on either side of the door. As the door opened she had an impression of dark woods with high finishes, white walls, the occasional perfect object precisely placed. James met them, introducing himself to the children with great gravity. He was so trim and graceful in his white duck trousers that Nan felt at once twenty pounds heavier; she imagined her hips bumping against doorframes as she moved on through the hall into the living room.

"Hello, darling, my Hollandaise won't Hollandaise," Mr. Rabbit said; he was still holding a dripping whisk.

"Tad, Jake, this is Mr. *Abbott*," she said firmly; they both looked so disappointed that she knew they had half expected their host to be a dressed-up bunny rabbit with wire-framed glasses, vest, watch and chain. She pushed them forward, saying, as if she needed to explain: "That's Tad and this is Jake. These are my boys."

"Oh," he said, and she saw that he was drunk, "you brought them. Heaven only knows what they're going to eat."

"This is the terrace," James said tactfully, "maybe the boys would like to play on the swing."

"Anything will do." She saw the children fanning out, looking for signs of a party; if this was a party, where was the cake?

"I only made enough crabmeat salad for us-all, and the poor things would hate it anyway."

"Peanut butter," she said hastily, thinking if she had more character she would grab her boys and run for safety, but she was aware of the other guests, blurring at the edges of the room. "Tuna fish. Look boys, there's the terrace. You can play outside."

"You've already met Edward Claren and this is Mrs. Claren." James had taken her hand and was trying to draw her into the group.

"Look," she said in an undertone, "maybe it would be better if. . . ."

"Don't worry, Emmett always goes to pieces when he cooks." James went on to introduce her to Miss Brill and her student, a raw-looking high school boy who had won two poetry prizes and had a poem coming out in *The Atlantic* some time soon; Emmett was going to give him a few pointers later because he used to be a writer in New York before he came up here to live. The boy looked miserable and Nan thought: In over his head. She wanted to sit down and draw him out, but James was pulling her along. The boy's eyes met hers for a second; he grimaced as at a fellow victim and there was no way for Nan to let him know that it was more complicated than that, she was no victim, she might even be able to help him feel secure and adult in this prickly group. As she turned she wrote the fantasy in which she became his mistress and mentor and then freed him to live his own life; smiled at it, set it aside and went on to say a polite how-do-you-do to Edward Claren's mother, who was being not so much reintroduced by her son as conferred upon Nan, rather like the Legion of Merit. Edward finished in a pink flush and sat down, and because she had no choice Nan took the chair at Mother's side. Mother's monologue had no pauses and so Nan was able to say, "Mmmm," watching as James followed Mr. Rabbit into the kitchen, thinking this might even work out; she was going to have a good time.

The others were a durable divorcee in a splashy print and the town librarian, who pressed weights and ran with the high school kids. Another man came downstairs, but James didn't bother to introduce him; although he first-named everybody, they all called him Reynolds, which could have been a first name or a last. His position in the household was never specified, but Nan decided at last that he must be a paying guest, and couldn't help but wonder if this summer was turning out to be everything his travel agent had led him to expect. The room was graceful, all the guests were scrubbed, tanned and attractive, but as Nan followed the chains of insult and allusion she understood that she didn't belong here, at least not yet; even Reynolds seemed to be more at home here than she was; like Miss Brill's student, she was here on trial.

She had been aware for some minutes of her own boys' voices rising, and with them, the level of their activity; there seemed to be twice as many bumps and shouts, a geometric progression of footsteps. They were going to reach critical mass soon; she could tell by the slant of sunlight that it was past their suppertime and so, excusing herself, she went to the terrace door with a dish of nuts. Both boys pounced like little savages and she heard in the room behind her, "Aren't they cute," and, "Adorable," words with an edge, and thought the best thing would be to feed them fast and put them to bed in an upstairs room where nobody could hurt them.

She walked into a quarrel in the kitchen. James looked at her in some relief, thinking perhaps Emmett would stop when he saw her, but instead he said, "You always would hide behind women."

Nan's instinct was to flee but James had taken her hand, saying, "What can we do for you?"

"Peanut butter."

Mr. Rabbit was saying, "You always have been a tasteless weakling."

James looked nonplussed but held tight to her hand. "Peanut butter?"

"You know, something for the children."

"If you had any guts at all you wouldn't be trapped in this jerkwater town. Say you're sorry."

James said hurriedly, "I think we have some graham crackers and I could butter them. Would that do?"

"I said, apologize."

The children hated graham crackers, but Nan would have said anything to get away. "That would be wonderful."

"James, I'm speaking to you."

"All right," James said, close to tears. "Whatever it was, I'm sorry, I'm very, very sorry."

"And you'll never do it again."

His face was rippling under the strain but at last he said, wearily, "And I'll never do it again."

"Very well." Satisfied, Emmett took a tray of canapes into the living room.

Nan would never have asked: Why?

But James was pulling two stools over to the counter, saying,

"When I first came here, I lived in an efficiency." He set two saucers on the counter and began making cracker sandwiches, adding three cherry tomatoes to each child's plate. He went on, not necessarily for her, but for himself: "In the winters I could go for a whole weekend, Friday night to Monday, without hearing another human voice."

"I'll go get the children." Nan turned to look directly at him. "Look, I'm sorry if they've turned this into a mess. . . ."

"Don't be silly, we're delighted to have them." James was pouring milk into two sherry glasses. "The little one has a very sweet face."

When she went back to the terrace Tad grabbed her around the knees, too tight, and Jake hugged her flank and whatever other parts of her he could encompass. Everybody in the living room wanted to be introduced, they wanted to shake hands and pat and prod, asking the boys all those simple-minded questions put by people who don't know children, but Nan protected them, standing in the doorway with her hands on their shoulders, saying, "This is Tad and that's Jake, they're going to have their supper now."

Tad broke from her and started toward the kitchen, tripping on a prayer rug and falling full length. She knew he hadn't hurt himself, but he screamed and when she picked him up he cried as if pushed to the limit, and they both knew it wasn't about the bump or because there weren't any rabbits, it wasn't even because there wasn't going to be any cake; she sat down on the floor with Tad in her lap, and when James popped out of the kitchen, anxious to help, she drove him back with a savage look. She held Tad tight long after he had stopped crying, and when her own face had cleared she took him into the kitchen, thinking the sooner she had them safe in bed upstairs the better off they'd be. By the time she woke them up to take them home they would be renewed, this would be an adventure again. They could run ahead of her, drunk on moonlight and capering in the fields. If she came again, she would find a way to leave them home.

When the boys wouldn't eat the graham crackers she let them

each take a piece of bread upstairs, smiling in vindictive satisfaction as she watched them curl up with their sneakers and their bread crusts on Mr. Rabbit's bed. She kissed them both and promised them a bakery cake first thing tomorrow, they would have a party on the hotel porch.

By the time she reached the living room, shadows were collecting in all the corners, rolling out to envelop the guests. Emmett was leaning against a bookshelf next to the tray of canapes, which he had forgotten to pass. The cocktail hour had already gone on for too long and Nan thought with a twinge of despair that they might have to go on having drinks forever because Emmett was already too drunk to lay the meal he had spent all day preparing. She thought briefly of going to the kitchen and falling on the children's graham crackers, but James had rescued her drink from the spot next to Edward Claren's mother, and he sat her down between himself and Miles, who had been divorced twice and was explaining at length why marriage was a drag and how important it was to have a circle of friends to turn to, different people for different things. James said he thought that was shallow and as the two of them rattled on, Nan was delighted to be picking up lines and building on them. It was a relief to be dealing in subtleties after what seemed like months of talking to nobody but little boys; it was fun to be somewhere where she could be accepted for herself. Miss Brill turned out to be funnier than seemed possible on first sight, and, separated from his mother, Edward Claren had a gentle wit. By the time Nan looked up again it was almost dark in the room and she knew she was drunk.

She had been alerted by a funny silence, not just a pause between words but an uncomfortable, palpable thing of itself. Emmett had put a question and now the others were all looking at Miss Brill's student, waiting.

After too long the boy managed to say: "I . . . uh, I just write when I feel like it, I guess."

"Hah." Emmett pounced. "You'll never get anywhere that way."

The boy was ready to let it go at that. "Uh, maybe not."

"You'll never know anything about writing."

Nan heard herself saying, "Hey, wait a minute," but nobody heard.

Emmett went on. "As a matter of fact, I don't know why I invited you."

"*I* invited him," Miss Brill said. "Civilizing influence. You know."

"Hey." Nan looked to James, but he was smiling as blandly as all the others; he was not going to stop it. He knew better than to try and stop it.

Emmett was saying, "He still has dirt between his toes."

Miss Brill said, "That's hardly my fault."

The boy was writhing in his chair.

"I'm sorry," Nan said, standing up. "If I don't eat I'm going to die."

Emmett snapped, "In a *minute.*"

James was saying, "Relax, dear, we have hours."

"It's *late.*" Nan looked around for some ally and saw that they all knew it was getting late and were beyond caring; this was what they did every summer, and so long as they could collect here, it didn't really matter that there was always at least one fight before dinner, which was always late. Strays all, they had found their own specific for loneliness, and at the moment they were ready to receive her; hadn't she bustled the children through with a minimum of bother, hadn't she stashed them upstairs, out of sight?

Miles was saying, "Soon, dear. Soon."

Emmett said with mock weariness, "I suppose we'll have to feed this boy."

"I'm sorry," Nan said, and could not be sure whether it was their bitchiness she resented, or rather, their welcome. She stopped in front of her host. "You were never Mr. Rabbit. I'm going home."

Academic Novel

They live the life of the mind.

At a point somewhere outside the sequence, eight of the faculty leave this particular small university, or large college, to found the New Jerusalem. They are deserting the scene as the principals know it, but the academics who stay behind will follow their fortunes as if reading clues to their own futures.

The principals in the sequence, including Anand and Perdia, go out to wave them off: Goodbye!

The air is quick with adventure. There they go—four ambitious academic families with their treasures stuffed in U-Hauls, hopeful professors going by twos like animals into the ark, off to Vermont to found an experimental college. Anand wonders if by staying behind he has made a mistake.

Pioneers from faculties all over the country join the brave in the New Jerusalem, while back at the small university, or large college, Anand fluffs up his bibliography and awaits the call from Yale. His wife Perdia is not part of the scene, Anand thinks; after all, she is a nurse and by no means his intellectual equal.

But she belongs in the sequence because she is married to

Anand. Even though Anand is a rat, she persists. After all, she loves him.

Professors send joyous reports from the New Jerusalem: this is nothing like school. In the New Jerusalem, thinkers look for truth in a communal garden. When the sun gets too hot on their backs they take off their shirts: men, women, peacefully working together. Hopeful thinkers lie in pinwheels on the greensward with their feet pointed outward and their arms locked so that their heads touch, looking like great squirming anemones when all the time they imagine themselves as radiant, multifaceted, living stars.

Those who are left behind have to wonder, Do we lack drive and vision? Are we inflexible and what does it say about us, really? That we've lost sight of the future?

How are PhDs supposed to know that when you are too close to what you're doing, you can't necessarily discern the pattern?

Why, here at home in the old university, more traditional scholars stick to hoeing narrow rows; this lets them dig deep and explore thoroughly. Fowler, for instance, is busy finding out more than you want to know about the most boring parts of the eighteenth century. Anand's specialty is the captivity narrative. He would give anything to be an early American.

On other fronts Axel Foster and Vera Preston would kill to be named dean and Elfington is terrified that he won't get tenure. The archaeologists want to secede from Classics. Life's big moments are spun out in committees. The only major scenes take place in meetings and they exist to be written down by whoever's taking notes.

People who live in books have to go elsewhere for excitement.

The astonishment in the New Jerusalem—tales brought back by sailors—is in the number of subsequent divorces.

But their story unfolds outside the sequence.

The real story is back home in the university, where the old rules pertain. Life in the old place follows more logical lines, although professors sit up nights arguing: what is logic?

Within the sequence and only peripherally affected by the exodus—the pioneers have escaped!—the ambitious Anand is restless.

In Hyderabad the one-eyed man would be king, but in this country Anand is just another American Studies person—with a hitch. People say, You say you teach American literature and you don't even know American? Tears stand in his eyes, he who never read the funnies or watched "The Brady Bunch" until he got to the States, "I do, I do!" But how can he? Not fair, but fair. Poor Anand. There are no livings to be made here on the literature in Tamil or Urdu.

He spends too much on his clothes.

Although Perdia adores him, Anand looks for romance in expensive clubs and French restaurants, in the shoe department at Gucci and in gold chains from Cartier.

Perdia pretends she doesn't know he is unfaithful. How glamorous they look, riding around with the tops down on their little foreign cars with their Afghan stuffed in the back with its ears streaming like a woman's curls. This is in the year of dancing and petty flirtation, which followed the year of clever little dinners for eight and preceded the year of aggressively happy marriages.

The sequence?

Yes there is one—Punch to Judy, point A to Point B, cause and effect, although PhDs are sometimes too close to know which is which and none of us is able to discern the pattern.

Certainly one of the constant figures is Perdia, who will not find out for three more years that she is dying. She thinks it's unhappiness that makes her wake up feeling ill.

The other figures are respectively variable and constant. It is not easy to tell which are which, or to know whether the principals feel any responsibility to their designations.

We who are on the scene but are not among the principals, observe, or is it try to divine, the scheme. Although change is all around us, we personally choose to think of ourselves as constant.

This story is happening to everybody else! Untouched, we personally are only reading the endless novel this academic community is writing. How are PhDs supposed to know that when you are too close to what you're doing, you can't necessarily discern the pattern?

Perdia is older: no one knows how much—older than we are, older than the other principals. Specifically, she's older than Anand, her first and insofar as we know, only husband.

He has always treated her badly. It is Anand who brought her to this tiny academic community from downtown Manhattan, where she used to be a model, and Anand who reduces her to tears so often, usually just before or during some big party: pretty Perdia in her overdone getup with her iridescent lipstick glazed with swallowed tears and mascara streaking her beginning wrinkles.

Although Anand goes on to other pastures with the Other Woman, Perdia still cries and schemes to get him back. She will have affairs to prove to Anand that she is desirable.

Stocky, hairy Hunnage collects handguns. Even his girl-friends don't know that on nights when he's alone he sleeps with an automatic under his pillow. Not because he is afraid of intruders; no. He takes guns to bed as other people sleep with lovers—the pressure of smooth metal against his cheek.

The dean, who is not long for the job, also sleeps with a weapon—a butcher knife, because he is afraid of students. Predatory Axel Foster stalks him; at the first sign of weakness Axel will take his job away from him. Unless Vera Preston beats him to it.

———————

In this same period, also within the sequence, poor Fowler's wife runs away with a sophomore. She is a vivid, discontented, leggy girl who never looks the same twice—either because she hasn't decided who she is or has decided, but can't make the image hold still for her. The sophomore was one of Fowler's banner students. Nobody can quite remember him. Fowler lets his hair grow; it makes him look not trendy, but seedy and rootless, like a bag person at the full moon, the Wolfman in the first stages of the change.

Fowler's loss takes place before the year of oriental rugs but after the year of dancing and petty flirtation. Perdia and Anand are still married.

———————

Baba is losing her husband Lawrence; no problem. She throws herself into social work; sometimes addicts come to the house and stay for days, until she thinks they're detoxified. Never mind what they shoot or snort or pop when her back is turned; she reads recovery in their blurry eyes, a new lucidity. She is bent on helping them. Two or three months before the divorce Fred reports that in the depths of one hard night, a sniffling, shuddering teenaged addict comes to the house; he is so cold that Baba warms him, putting him in the bed between them.

Even as Perdia pretends ignorance of Anand's affairs, it is Perdia who forestalls Axel Foster, who although he is a French professor with exquisite pronunciation, is quite large. He used to be a Green Beret. Gradually Foster understands that his wife Marva is being unfaithful to him while he's away at meetings about the succession to the deanship. Axel pretends to be gone overnight and then sneaks back on his belly and spies on his house. You bet Marva is being unfaithful. Outraged, he goes looking for Anand.

He turns up on Perdia's doorstep at midnight: "Where is he?" In spite of Axel's battle training and her own relatively slight stature, pretty Perida bars the door with her frail body because she loves Anand and Axel wants to shoot him.

The next morning Axel Foster walks into the science building between classes—*between classes!* and beats the shit out of the astounded Glenn Jansen, Distinguished Professor of Chemistry, who is Anand's same height and stature. In front of witnesses, Foster almost throws him out the window. So much for the deanship.

Although poor Glenn is apparently not the adulterer, in the dark he really looks like Anand; there is also the tenor of the times—this is in the year of big, ugly parties, when anything can happen. He does not yet know his life is ruined.

Even Jansen's wife becomes suspicious. While poor Glenn is still in the hospital, she finds it necessary to go to the president's office and announce that it was a terrible mistake, her Glenn was home with her that night and has never, ever been unfaithful.

Innocent as he is, poor Glenn is changed by this mystifying, violent encounter. His hair turns white; his major experiment fizzles and although he and his wife are often seen kissing publicly, their marriage has never been the same.

"It's not what you're doing, it's what people *think* you're doing that makes all the difference," he tells his students every September, without explaining. Although he keeps himself neat and still smiles and goes among the people, poor Glenn is to all intents and purposes a broken man.

Anand leaves Perdia, but not for Marva Foster. All along he has been seeing a waitress in the Starlite Lounge at the local Hyatt. He drills her in correct English and buys her a new wardrobe before he introduces her to the scene.

This is in the year of big, ugly parties, which preceded the year of impulse purchases at auctions and the rolling poker game.

Although we live the life of the mind, we are engrossed, no, enthralled by the physical.

Look at us, professors all, studying life at one remove; physical scientists examining what exists, math people positing theories on the backs of theories built by others; linguists memorizing extant languages without the power to contribute to them, critics preparing to autopsy the works of writers; art historians dealing with art they have no real part in.

Who would not want to plunge into one of the few things an academic can experience directly? For in the absence of art there's always life, and PhDs don't necessarily know that when you are too close to what you're doing, you can't necessarily discern the pattern.

A student who lives with the Bennetts in this particular year says, "Until I moved in with you I thought professors were— just—like—*doctors.*"

Fowler's wife comes back. Alone in Canada with her sophomore, exhausted and sated, she found they had nothing to say to each other. It was not so much a matter of ignorance, she says, as lack of experience. Now she sits around the house and lets her hair get dirty. Poor Fowler.

Although nobody knows what's going on in his life, Hunnage has written a fellow professor wintering in England to find out if he knows of a field near the university where there are no trees to get in the way and no police ever come. Are we entering a duel situation? Is Hunnage the go-between or one of the duelists?

With Anand gone, pretty, wounded Perdia has taken a lover. His name is Federico and he has wavy hair and romantic brown eyes, although something—the set of the big head on the shoulders, perhaps, gives him a vulpine slouch. After the divorce she picked up Federico on a get-well trip to Milan, and she shows him to the others with the same pride with which she produces the beautiful knits, the handmade Italian boots and the blown glass she bought on the same trip. Federico, however, is duty-free. He is small-boned but beautifully set up, as if while Perdia sleeps he secretly works out.

Federico moves among us without being *of* us. A gay friend from the city spots Federico at one of our gatherings and is astounded: what is *that* doing at a party like *this?* It's as if he's spotted a boa in the dovecote where the hens preen without any apparent sense of danger.

Some of the women think Perdia is flaunting her lover—all of Europe's treasures theirs to admire, even to touch but not take home because unlike Perdia they must please the professor on the hearth. Some are grateful to have poor Perdia taken care of, because their own professors like to flirt at parties, and have roving eyes.

The women who are also professors are divided: they either flirt at parties to show how free they are, or disdain flirting, which they say is counterproductive. Love sits uneasily in these two-professor marriages, where life and work run at cross-purposes; are we colleagues here, or only lovers?

Whatever their underlying motives, the women are on the whole happy for Perdia. In view of what Anand did to her, it seems only right and fair. Federico is just the right height for her. He has a dirty grin. Is it Perdia's fault that there is a little voice inside of even the best of them, crying out, *my turn?*

Meanwhile Baba, who does her work principally in the definition of sex roles in early childhood behavior, appears to be in love with one of her bikers. She says she began what she calls the dialogues with him as part of her ongoing project, which has rushed in to fill the time she used to spend on being married. On his divorce lawyer's advice Lawrence has finally moved out, but he still comes home for changes of clothes and to take showers. He's confided to Hunnage that he can't be sure that it's only *a* biker and not *some* bikers.

Although the year of big, ugly parties is over and we like to spend our weekends at auctions, Baba gives a big, messy party to celebrate her divorce. It is the first of a series that we will go to over the years, before we tire of the Baba scene and stop going. She is a wonderful hostess, energetic and generous, but wearying; these things always end with Baba sitting on the piano and crying because she doesn't have a man.

The divorce party, however, is special because it marks Federico's debut. Perdia gives him free rein because she knows he's *not like us* and she's anxious to have him accepted. In spite of the language barrier he's doing fine. Every time we look up he's whispering romantically with someone new in a different corner.

Who wants to explain why three of the women guests and two men take stations on the nearby ski slopes the next afternoon, expecting to rendezvous with Federico in spite of the fact that they are betraying Perdia? Dusk will turn the frozen slopes purple before the would-be lovers give up on him and straggle down to the parking lot. When they first recognize each other and look away, abashed but determined to wait for him, Federico is far away. Perdia has him in New York in the men's department at Altman's, where to please her, he will try on several sport coats too conservative to amuse him.

Later we hear that Federico has married an American woman, to extend his visa. Perdia is devoted to him but no fool; she says he offered her first refusal but she prefers to keep her options open. She means that if she stays single, maybe Anand will come back to her. Can we help it if he and the Other Woman have a baby together in, where is it they went, Omaha, and Perdia can't bring herself to take off the chain Anand gave her, or her old wedding ring?

Besides, she says, back in Italy, Federico is already married and has five children.

Rheingold, who used to teach here, comes home in the middle of one slate-colored English winter day in Oxford to discover the mother of his children in bed with another woman.

Is there a significance or a function to gossip? Perhaps this is not a saga the university community is writing, but the funnies. The stories don't have much dignity; instead what we have here is the comic book the survivors read to pass the time in the stilly fastness of winter. Each spring we discover a new chapter has emerged—this affair revealed, that festering marriage lanced. In separate living rooms, the wounded partners sob out their stories.

Imagine what Vermont winters must be like in the New Jerusalem, where our splinter group has formed its experimental college.

We go to a housewarming in a deconsecrated church, with wine and seven-grain bread made by the couple who live there; it gets late and their infant runs at full speed up and down the altar platform, colliding occasionally with people's legs. He's exhausted and begging to be put to bed but on the whole, we are permissive parents.

There are rock music and dancing and orotund blessings by the theology professor who used to be a minister, while outside in the dark his own wife runs barefoot down the road in her white Mexican wedding dress. Nobody knows why, but we think she's crying.

———————

Is there a theory or a theorem that expresses this sequence? Is there a logic or a rhetoric that embraces this behavior?

Sometimes the sequence seems like an orderly temporal progress from cradle to grave, from point A to point B—or an intellectual one, from ignorance to bliss.

At others, it is not linear but cyclical, not cyclical but parabolic, a series of exits and returns so dizzying and brilliant that it's hard to keep track of the players and impossible to tell who are friends and who are enemies, or which of the characters are good and which are bad.

Of course this changes.

In this respect the university is like the evening TV soaps, in which there can be no clear dichotomy of good and evil and no final definition of a character as either one—for in the university there is always the possibility of deathbed conversion and the imminent danger of an unexpected fall from grace.

———————

Academics are dreamers, not well organized enough to nail the bad guy in the act and have him put away for what he's doing. They can't even decide who the bad guy is. Confronted with an axe murder, they will vote to discuss the implications at a meeting.

This sordid discovery comes after the community has become so large that the years pass without any specific characterization. The last designated year we remember—when the community was small enough to act as a unit—was the year of saunas and running, which immediately followed the year of being happily married: couples openly snuggling at parties, uxorious, aggressively *together.*

When the Bennetts, professors both, decide to get divorced, each does what any sober academic would do. They tell their respective department chairs before they break the news to the children. Although their arguments are bitter, bitter, neither of them wants to do anything unseemly. Next they make appointments with the provost and the college president. Then they put an all-campus memo on the electronic bulletin board, where it will be available to the fellow faculty members who have in fact managed to master their computers.

The divorcing Rheingolds, on the other hand, intend to stay friends. They write friendly letters to close colleagues saying they are still fond of each other but they find it necessary to keep pace with the changing times. We find out later that what they mean is that she's fallen in love with a stewardess and he's in love with an actress. They cite self-realization, or is it self-fulfillment, among other things; they say they feel no guilt.

They ask us what's the matter with *us*, that we aren't out there on the front lines along with them.

In this context the Bennetts' reserved, academic approach is somewhat refreshing.

Perdia gets a letter from Federico, who has been deported. She is impressed by the letterhead: *Castello Regina Coeli.* Although she thinks she's a realist, she's certain he's landed among the gentry until this sad note, at the bottom of the handwritten letter, disabuses her: "I am tired of jail."

In some ways Perdia is glad her lover is far away, so he won't have to see what's become of her body. By this time her illness has been diagnosed. Although the prognosis is death, doctors will alternately maim her and poison her in an attempt to cure her.

Still, Perdia is gallant in pretty clothes with coordinated jewelry, careful makeup; sensitive treatment of the hair, which for the first time since we've known her, goes from platinum back to natural grey, which makes us sad. Dying, she is beautiful. Suffering burns out the consequences of all her follies.

———————

Fothing the paranoid anthropologist is discovered at the Chateau Frontenac; he has a Rolls Royce outside with the motor running. His checks are all bouncing; they're springing around the hotel lobby like released butterflies, which prompts the anxious desk clerk to call the provost and the college president. In the absence of Fothing's family and friends, they are designated the responsible parties. In the trunk of the Rolls, police have found a snorkel mask and a thicket of stolen billiard cues.

———————

And this isn't the half of it.

———————

Staring at the tracks our lives have made, we in the university community try to understand what informs the sequence, what separates and what links us. This is the question raised in *The Bridge of San Luis Rey*—what links these lives? Is there really a bridge here and are we really on it? Close as we are to what's going on, blind and confused and moving along without knowing whether we are in fact going forward, we who are on the scene but outside the sequence look at our mingled lives and try to discern a pattern.

It's better not to dwell on the children in the community; some are badly damaged and others are fine and still others bear no resemblance to the fathers whose names they carry. One or two look curiously like Anand, although Perdia will not hear a word said against him.

On her deathbed, which approaches faster than any of us could have anticipated, Perdia will reveal her biggest secret. If it does not explain everything that's happened here, then it illuminates at least some of it.

We gather in her room, holding flowers, some of us, candy, new bedroom slippers, tokens to take her mind off dying. Her eyes are not fixed on us, or even on the hereafter.

As some of us bend near, she whispers: "You know Axel Foster? When he hit Glenn Jansen because he thought he was Marva's lover? It was really Anand. When Axel came looking for Anand I just couldn't tell him. I said it was Glen."

There is matter caught in one of the tubes that carries wastes from her kidney, but this is less important to her than what she is trying to tell us.

"I had to lie to Axel. Of course I lied," she says, when some of us find this disconcerting—poor Glenn! Ruined by a case of mistaken identity! "Listen, he had a gun," Perdia says, but that isn't it. She finishes with the truth. "I love Anand. I would do anything to keep Axel from hurting him."

We are introduced to the concept of negative proof. By identifying certain points on the perimeter, it is possible to prove that we've traveled certain roads to specific intersections in the city without having to give away any sensitive information. It is a theory most of us understand only sometimes, grasping it whole in an intuitive flash and in the next second watching comprehension flee and with it the theory; we see it receding, winking like the white tail of a deer escaping into an impenetrable forest.

How are PhDs supposed to know that when you are too close to what you're doing, you can't necessarily discern the pattern?

Perdia is in the hospital for the last time; because she is so sick we'll only see her once or twice in the last days, but we all think about her. Recovered from his betrayal by his wife, Rheingold has come back from England with a Welsh girl he introduces to all of us. The actress, he says; he says she can't live without him. It seems important to him to make us understand that although his wife sought satisfaction with another woman, he is an insatiable and successful lover.

Hunnage is discovered on an airplane going to a scholarly convention with his bow tie askew and his swimming-pool eyes glaring as if snapped open by the blaze of a flashbulb; there is an automatic tucked into his belt but he doesn't even know it. Somewhere in the throat, he's begun to hemorrhage, and we don't have the foggiest idea which of the many drugs he abuses has done this to him.

Fowler has left his wife and moved in with Baba.

And the bridge?

The bridge is less likely to be love than passion. Unless it is fear, or anxiety, or madness. Academics, no, theoreticians spend whole lifetimes at one remove from the original artifact.

Is the sequence their attempt to grapple hand-to-hand with experience?

Or is it only our attempt to understand it?

———————

Leached white and burned away to the bone, purified and preparing to leave us, Perdia contemplates her life—the liaisons, the comic triumph with Federico. And Anand? After everything, even dying, Perdia still loves him. And the bridge? She will tell you that it is love and we are too sensitive and bemused and, yes, too hopeful to refute her.

———————

Uncertain and urgent and somehow bereft, we contemplate the sequence.

It is everything, whether or not we understand it.

Victory Dreams

"Where do you think Daddy is now, Grandmother?"

"When it's safe for them to tell us, we'll know." Grandmother Hess was driving her to the dispensary, trim old lady in her navy blue gabardine, with her steely hair wound in a tight roll. Her carriage was erect; she might have been an office in a branch of the service which existed but had not yet been named. She exuded calm, which was one reason Mary Kay had begun. Grandmother Hess quieted fears with a calm word. She was proof against panic; she would face air raids, invasion, mortal combat with monumental calm.

The girl needed reassurance this morning, not only for Daddy's sake. There was something wrong with her insides and she was scared. They were going to the Navy doctor to find out what. "Do you think his ship is out there alone?"

"Of course not. They would be in a task force, under escort."

Her appointment was at eleven. "I wish he was here."

"You know he has a job to do." Grandmother had hesitated at the gate; she was waiting for the sentry to pass her through. "We can't always have what we want when we want it, Mary Kay."

She was upset and knew it, badgering her grandmother. "Do you really think he'll be all right?"

"Stop that!"

Her voice was like a querulous child's. "Promise he's all right."

"Don't you play that game with me."

Grandmother had stopped in front of the dispensary. Loved or not loved, forgiven or not, Mary Kay was going to have to go inside. At fourteen, after two years, she had started missing periods. The first she barely noticed; the second troubled her, where was it, she let it go by. When she missed the third she got scared. If she could hide it from Grandmother maybe it would get better all by itself, but this was too much to deal with alone, so last night she told Grandmother and here they were. She didn't know what she had expected: to get Daddy home from the Pacific? To be reassured? What she had not expected was the terrifying look of alarm, the curt efficiency, the speed with which Grandmother had brought her here. Did she have cancer? She could not help wondering whether she was dying, and if so, of what.

"Do you want me to come in with you?"

Of course she did, but Grandmother had her jaw set, and this was all so embarrassing that Mary Kay said, "It's OK."

"All right. I'll wait here."

Mary Kay could not get out of the car. "Oh Grandmother, what's the *matter* with me?"

Grandmother looked like General MacArthur right now, carved out of stone. "Hurry along."

"You don't think it's. . . . Ah. Cancer?"

"The only thing that makes a woman miss her period is getting pregnant," her grandmother said grimly. "Now you go on in."

"I'm only in the ninth grade."

Her grandmother faced front, saying in a tone that struck terror, "It's happened to other girls your age."

Oh my God, she thought. *Maybe I am. But how?* If Grandmother said so, she thought in the terrible purity of childhood ignorance, it must be true. Maybe she had used a toilet after a boy or accidentally used one of their towels. Grandmother knew, she thought in her horrendous innocence; she was usually right. Muddy had never told her anything and she couldn't figure out everything from books; now Grandmother said there could only be one reason for the thing that had happened to her and she sat in the waiting room trying to decide: baby or cancer, which one would be worse? She started praying: I will eat vomit if you'll just make it all right, I'll never have another piece of candy in my life. She was sick, trembling in an orgy of fear and ignorance so that when it was her turn to go into the examining room she burst into tears at the doctor's first question, answering like a child: "I feel bad."

After she calmed down she told him what was the matter without saying what she was really afraid of: Grandmother. When he said missing periods was perfectly normal in girls her age, a simple hormonal fluke, Mary Kay cried for so long that he prescribed something for her nerves. Then he had her sit in the waiting room until she was herself again, and she was so relieved that she kept on crying, not hysterically, just quietly, sitting on the cracked leatherette sofa with the tears running down her cheeks. She was not like Muddy after all, no cancer, no rotting from the inside out. She was not like Muddy in any other way. Grandmother was in the waiting room too, she sprang on the doctor as he led Mary Kay out. She supposed she ought to go over and listen to the two of them but she was grateful to the doctor for being there to deal with Grandmother; let him explain.

Leaving the dispensary, Grandmother mumbled a few hurried words that Mary Kay didn't try to hear. Later in life when she understood the shape and size of the wrong that had been done her, the failure of trust, she would not remember whether her grandmother was admitting this or trying to apologize. What she would remember was the two of them heading for a soda fountain where Grandmother bought her a sundae—to celebrate? To make up for it? She would remember Grandmother talking about her life.

"I come from a long line of Navy wives," she said, as if nothing had happened today. "Your Great-great-grandfather Britton sailed out of New Bedford on a whaler. Your Great-grandfather Rice served in an ironclad. He fought in the Civil War. They both came back."

"But Grandfather didn't come back."

"Your father never saw me shed a tear."

"But you ought to be able to cry." Otherwise it went unmarked. Was she talking about Grandfather, or the dispensary?

"It's important to carry on." Grandmother Hess loathed desserts but here she was poking at an ice-cream soda and looking around, as if for something more to give. "My father was at sea for so long I forgot what he looked like. We lived in Georgetown and even when I prayed for him I could never remember his face. When I closed my eyes it was his picture I saw, and not my father at all."

I will never forget my father.

"When he came back I was so jealous that I hid in the closet and cried." Grandmother tied her soda straw in a knot without even noticing. "Then he was transferred to the War College and he moved us here."

Her mouth was watering. "And he came home every single night."

Then Grandmother Hess said the most surprising thing. "And I never forgave him for taking me away from Washington and all my friends. Of course you'd know better. And whatever happens, you'll carry on."

"But he is coming back, Grandmother."

Grandmother knew what Mary Kay was asking for, considered, and gave it to her. She managed to look like a figurehead and an admiral at the same time. "If anybody comes back, your father will."

The girl could not have said precisely what happened next but would remember it as a *click*, some mysterious internal adjustment, as of an element of destiny snapping into place. She would remember thinking: *There.*

She sealed it. "Then all we have to do is wait."

They were home in time for the noon news. Afterward Grandmother would go through the newspapers, clipping any references to Navy Air, the *Yorktown*. She was on her second scrapbook and at dinner would lay out the map, trying to piece together what she read and what she heard on the news.

Mary Kay had been instructed by the radio, the newspapers, the magazines: keep it cheerful. *I am fine,* she wrote to her father. *The flowers are up so I guess spring is here.* She threw herself into the bond drive, the scrap drive, helped Grandmother bake for the servicemen's canteen. At night they closed the blackout curtains and went out to scan the water. If there were German subs in the waters off Newport, where would the Nazis come ashore? They did all these things without being sure precisely why; it had something to do with attention, or concentration. Even though the war was thousands of miles away they had to fight it here. If Muddy and the others had kept their minds on it maybe none of this would have happened; maybe nothing worse would happen if she could keep her mind on it. If she faltered for a second then the *Yorktown* might be torpedoed, or her father's plane ignited in the sky.

Dear Daddy,

Grandmother is a plane spotter now. I think she could pick out a Messerschmitt before anybody at the base. I am rolling bandages. Look for my initials on the end. I'm knitting something for you. It's guess what color. Navy blue.

She was knitting all the time now, socks and watch caps and sweaters to send her father, even though she didn't know if it was cold where he was. They fell from her needles like shells from an assembly line.

Mrs. McMurty is hoarding dogfood. Cans and cans of Pard. She says she is sending her meat ration coupons to the troops.

She wrote every week; she had to help him serve his country. He has served his country for as long as I can remember, she thought with a disloyal flicker; he was serving it before we even had the war. Was it to get away from us, she wondered, and amended it quickly: *from Muddy.* Then she put it out of her mind before it could hurt anything.

Keep 'em flying, Daddy, OK?

Now it seemed to her there were only the two of them: Muddy was gone, Daddy was gone. She could not have borne it if she had thought much about it; she refused to number all the changes but needed to signify them in some way.

All my love always, she signed herself in April, as ever, and then, recognizing all the changes—in her family, in herself—she wrote: *Kay Hess.*

From that day on she would sign herself Kay Hess; she was going to be just as assured and grown up as anybody else. There were stars and band leaders named Kay, she thought, cutting her hair and buying new sweaters. With minuscule changes, some delicate calibration, she could have been popular. As it was she managed all the externals, the angora sweater, the silver barrette, but when boys began to bump her in the halls and send her notes she never quite responded right because she was still caught and pulled along by the invisible current tugging underneath: Daddy. The war. I have to bring him back from the war.

For her fifteenth birthday she got an aqua sweater set from Grandmother, embroidered: *Kay.* To her astonishment her ailing mother sent her own Naval Academy miniature, that was her engagement ring. Kay loved it, wanted to be—what? At the Academy Ring Dance, with some beautiful, faceless Second Classman slipping on the ring. Daddy had written a Newport jeweler and there was a locket with a tiny diamond set in miniature wings. She felt disloyal for wanting to cry. When the war is over I'll never cry again.

When she cut the tiny cake her grandmother had made she discovered she was happy after all. My pretty sweaters, my locket, she thought. The cake and all. My ring. She could see her grandmother's hands moving, her expression: Grandmother would make a circus for Mary Kay if she had the power, she would wish the entire missing family in this room. "I have a batch of doughnuts for you to take to the canteen," she said, adding because it was all she had left to give: "If you want, you can stay and dance."

"Oh Grandmother."

"But only for an hour."

The servicemen's canteen was in a second-floor hall down the street. She could hear "Chattanooga Choo Choo" playing, found knots of sailors from the base standing by the coffee tables, a handful of Marines. There were only a few girls: somebody from her school and a few secretaries from the War College. The place was decorated with a couple of posters and a Coke sign, but she would not even notice the dirty plaster, the floorboards scored with grime. She saw only the boys, or were they men, and it may have been the danger and rush of wartime or only the uniforms, but they were all handsome or at least cute. The jukebox was playing "You'd Be So Nice to Come Home To," and the next thing she knew she was slow-dancing in the amber light.

The sailor wasn't any better a dancer than she was but he held her close with his sweaty chin against her forehead, dipping on every turn. They whirled in an orgy of concentration until somebody cut in.

It was a meat-faced Marine corporal who was so old that it frightened her; he moved off with such assurance that she did not question it. She forgot his face because he danced better than anybody outside the movies, leading her into steps she didn't know she knew. He led with the authority of a drill instructor and she gave her will to him in a kind of relief, following in the pleasure of the dance. Although she could not have known why, they moved as smoothly as accustomed lovers; with each new turn he tightened his arm and she followed as if they were one person, warming to him in spite of his forbidding manner, the ugly face. She could feel the warmth of his body along the length of hers, his firm arm at her back, his breath on her cheek. She did not know exactly what it was that left her sapped of will but did not want it to stop. She could have danced all night without protesting, would have danced with him there and in the street and wherever else they went, wanted to explore this feeling and expand it into—what? Instead at the end of the third record he released her and stood back with a scowl. He seemed to be judging, trying to decide: whether she was a good dancer? Whether she would make a good Marine?

"What grade are you in?"

His bark startled her into the truth. "Ninth."

"Well you don't belong here," he said and walked away.

She was about to cry when a new boy touched her arm. She might not suit some people but there were plenty of partners here. This sailor was a steelworker's son from Chicago and he promised they would win the war this year. He wanted to jitterbug and they could have been Andy Hardy and his girlfriend, getting ready for the big show. The next partner bent her back like Gene Kelly, or Fred Astaire. She was aware by this time that there were other boys waiting and still other boys gathering to watch, so she was dancing for all of them now, more and more strongly aware of her body in the twin sweaters, the swing of her skirt against her legs; she had more power than she had dreamed of, and, knowing, would never be the same.

"Hello, dreamboat."

"My name is Kay."

This one held her a little bit too close; was he a wolf? It didn't matter; she whirled, she could have been Scarlett O'Hara, the night of the ball. It was like being in the movies, she thought, feeling his hot breath in her ear, and when he asked her where they could go together she did not pull back in shock, partly because she did not understand what he wanted and partly because she liked the way it felt. She could imagine herself and some nice boy kissing in the moonlight, her first romance. So she found herself melting against this sailor that she hadn't even liked at first because of the hair tonic, and tiny moustache, responding to his fingers fumbling in the hair at the back of her neck. Even as she let him pull her closer, her front warm against his front, some inner sentry was awakening, and despite his silky touch she heard the words as clearly as if they had been spoken: the war; I have to because of the war.

"What's the matter?"

She had quite simply pulled away from him. "I just."

He pulled her back. "Baby?"

"My father is on the *Yorktown*." Maybe he didn't understand. "He's an officer."

"Mmm." Nothing happened; he had his face in her neck now going mmm and when she tried to pull away he would not let go. She was trapped here, locked tight, and she did not know what would have happened to her next if somebody hadn't tapped the sailor on the arm. He only held her tighter. "Shove off."

"Sailor, I outrank you."

"Sir?"

When he let go it was like taking off an overcoat; her whole front got cold. Her new partner was the meat-faced corporal; there was authority in every line of his compact body, and she wanted nothing more right now than to move into his arms and take up where they had left off. He whirled her out without speaking and she followed with her will ebbing, her strength going fast; she would do anything he wanted, she thought, which was why it was a shock when he released her suddenly, at the top of the stairs, and gave her a little shove.

"Go home."

"I wasn't doing anything."

"It's time for you to go home." He took her by the elbows and turned her, steering her down the steps and into the street.

"You don't belong here."

"I was only dancing." She was about to cry.

"If you're afraid to go by yourself I'll walk you. All right?" When she did not move he took her by the elbows, glowering. "You're a very pretty girl and you're too young for this. Now I want you to go home."

"What did you say?" *Did you say I was . . .*

"I said, go home." He started propelling her. "Now which one is your house?"

"This one," she said automatically, and let him put her on the doorstep. She was so taken up in what he'd said that she didn't even mind. *Pretty.*

He spoke to her sternly, as if to a child. "Now don't come back until you're older, understand?"

By the time Grandmother came down with her grey hair hanging, he had gone. She was livid, pulled Kay inside, saying through her teeth, "That's it. That's the last time. I only let you go because it was your birthday. The last time. Ever. Do you understand?"

"It's OK, it doesn't matter."

"And don't bother to beg."

"I said, it doesn't matter, Grandmother." It didn't, she realized. She was warm, giddy, confused; now she understood some of what had happened, what he had been trying to say; if she couldn't go back to the canteen she couldn't, she thought, and was relieved. *Pretty. Yes.* Thought of the vigil she was keeping. *Something I have to do.*

That night she lay in the blackness of her bedroom, flat on her back with her arms spread as if forever fixed in velvet at the bottom of the sky. In the next second she was both there in the darkness and flying far above it, bounded here by blazing stars and there by winking lights, whether of Newport or Pearl or Tokyo she could not say; she understood only his dazzling freedom in this vision of or from her father's plane.

Prisoner of War

When the pain closes its teeth in her loins, Nell Bidscombe circles back on the last time she was held prisoner, on the premise that escape is easy once you have established the route. Escape is important to her now, as the options the doctors present continue to narrow; soon there will be none.

But in childhood she and her big sister Jake brought it off; they did! As Nell sees it now they were practically prisoners of war in that terrible German convent. It was awful, they got out; they can do it again.

The seven-year-old Nell was wiry and resourceful and willing to try anything, and in her soul Nell knows that today she is that same person. When she looks in the mirror she sees herself looking out of that same face. In spite of the lifetime that has fallen in between, she and Jake are still those same little girls whose father was killed in the *Arizona*. When the war started they were both surprised.

On Koolhawe Drive in Honolulu when they were little, Nell and Jacqueline slept together on the *hikie* with stuffed Koalas and a doll in a hula skirt. Sunday nights they had waffles and cocoa and listened to Jack Benny with Mother and Daddy, and they were happy. Ordinary. Daddy let Nelly and Jake ride to the end of the drive on his running board and Mother bought them kimonos and starched Japanese *tabis* with the separated toe; they played house in a packing crate in the mountainside garden with the ships in the harbor glittering below. Mother made playhouse curtains out of checkered dish towels and they had a dog, but that was before the Japs bombed Pearl Harbor and Mother went off somewhere inside herself to grieve.

Without wanting to the Bidscombe girls quit being ordinary. They got turned into something else. In a misbegotten attempt at kindness, some friend of Mother's blundered in and laid waste their efforts to be brave and look normal, *normal*; she hugged them, blubbering: "Oh you poor children, you have lost your father." Nelly and Jake were doing all right. Why did this big lady have to make them cry? They could have stayed in Honolulu; they would have done fine; she didn't have to put them on the first transport back to the States.

Confused by the suddenness of change, the children spent their last ten nights in Honolulu in their quarters in the blackout, listening for discordant cries of the invaders, Japanese paratroopers crunching through the bushes to attack them, or the burr of returning planes. They and the Pottinger boys and the other children who had been gathered armed themselves; Nell clutched a Baby Ben alarm clock, ready to scale the enemy's body like a tree so she could smash his head. They sang.

On the second night, when the shore batteries boomed and Nelly started to cry, Jake reached into the shadows that cluttered the dark bedroom and pulled out the story of the Red Line.

"The Red Line cuts through the darkness and sometimes we see it," Jake began, drawing an imaginary line across the center of the room for them. Nelly saw it as clearly as if she'd done it with paint. "And sometimes we go across."

The Red Line fell between the children and the bedroom door in the darkened quarters on Koolhawe Drive. Wonderful stories unfolded on the other side. On the other side of the line they were protected, safe from the Boogey Man, from Japs, from further accidents and surprises. Once Jake drew the Red Line, everything shifted: the world, the way they lived in the world.

It is this invention Nell hopes to recreate; if the Red Line does not mark an actual escape route for her, it is at least a starting point.

She's unclear about the mechanics of Jake's invention but Nell thinks that crossing the Red Line, you turned into your mirror image; with everything so changed, all things were possible. They could have made a mistake about Daddy. While she and Jake scrunched in the dark with the Pottingers, making up stories, the Navy could be out there in a diving bell, finding him. Even today Nell wears the same old look of trust and bewilderment. On some metaphysical plane she still believes Daddy is safe, in an air-filled chamber somewhere deep inside the *Arizona*, on a remote island—somewhere, waiting to be restored to her.

Therefore she has grown up not so much bereft as tentative and expectant. Hopeful. It was not a matter of what *happened*, exactly, that lifted Nell's heart and took her imagination; it was what *could* happen.

(Seeing her younger sister trapped in bed like this, in pain and with recovery by no means certain, the adult Jake crumples: "I wish I could help you."

As her insides knot, Nell says through her teeth, "Just sit here and help me wait for it to be over."

Does Jacqueline see her own death written in her younger sister's face? In her own obscene good health, does she feel guilty? "Be OK, OK?" Jake says, as if it's her own life she's pleading for.

Trapped in bed as she is in the room cluttered with prescription bottles, Nell wishes she and Jake could cross the Red Line together right now and have adventures. But for Nell the territory has become too private. She also knows that the visiting Jake is uncomfortable in the presence of her illness, which means Nell can't trust her to concentrate on the old story or remember it correctly. She hates seeing Jake so near tears.

When she can speak Nell says, "I'd love some coffee." She has to let Jake think she's helping. Besides, although she can't yet define the territory or pull her older sister into it, she knows she needs her if she's going to bring this off.

It was, after all, Jake who got them out of Mariagaard. She and Jake don't even like each other all the time, but they lived together in an orphanage after their father was killed in the *Arizona*; they survived on Koolhawe Drive in the first days of the war and later they escaped from Mariagaard, they did. Survivors of the same childhood, they are bonded. Are stronger. Escape artists. Masters at recovery.)

Today Nell does not remember what it was like on the other side of the Red Line, except that it was always safe, Daddy was fine and they had adventures. What she does remember is that in the black-out and on the boat going back to America and in the single room Mother rented in Washington, the Red Line shifted and became real. Nell could hardly wait for it to be night again. There was a different world on the other side, with rules suspended.

If not at ease with her illness, Nell is at least hopeful. It is only when she thinks about the long-ago taxi ride to Mariagaard that she shakes with grief: two little girls stuffed into a taxicab with their luggage and a note to the mother superior—Nelly and Jake, waving goodbye to Mother. They were so small: just seven and almost nine, two little girls packed off all alone for the Eastern Shore of Maryland.

Mother didn't even tell them ahead of time.

They just woke up one day and found Mother packing; they couldn't imagine why she was shoving wrapping paper into the toes of their school sandals this morning, fiercely jamming tissue paper into the freshly ironed puffed sleeves of their cotton dresses. Nell remembers tears—whose?—dissolving the pink tissue paper, Mother's fury because it stained one of the dresses: Look, she cried. Look what you did after everything I've done for you.

Mother is dead now, which does not end Nell's compulsion to turn it over and over in her mind: why Mother sent them away so completely. Widow like that with two little girls, insurance and a Navy widow's pension; she didn't have to make a career in retailing; she could have made a home instead, and her daughters? Brought halfway across the world on a Navy transport and across the continent by train, for what? To be dumped in boarding school, out of the way; couldn't Mother have done better?

What did she say when she bundled them into the taxi? "It's for the war effort. The bombers will never strike Chestertown."

The adult Nell charged Mother with it: *Why wouldn't you come with us?* Grappling with this, Nell understood why she'd found it so hard for her, not to love her own daughters, but to express it. "You should have kept us," she said, weeping.

"For God's sake, Nelly."

"Those poor little girls!"

"What about poor me?" her mother cried angrily. "I'm the one who had to earn a living."

It took Nell years of therapy to come to terms with the fact that Mother probably loved her daughters, but she never really liked them. In weak moments she wonders if it's undigested bitterness that's made her sick—or is it an insufficiency of love at a crucial stage in her life, some part of her body just letting go for lack of reinforcement? Yes she ignored her symptoms for too long. Did she hope they'd go away, or was it the need to demonstrate: *I told you something was wrong.* What was she doing, trying to get even?

Nell knows perfectly well that it's nature that makes people sick, the bacillus, the virus, the mutant gene, the act of God, and unlike the furniture inside her head, which can be rearranged, the path of her body's march through time is irreversible.

Still there are certain things she can do. Has done. Is doing. This: if she goes back now, and recovers it, she may be able to remember how she and Jake escaped the convent. She can escape this too; she knows it. Once you cross the Red Line, anything can happen.

She and Jake presented themselves at the convent door in patent leather shoes and party dresses—their best. They looked so nice; Nell was particularly proud of the lace on the cuffs of her white cotton socks. And the ribbon Mother had put on Kolie, her Koala. What did they think they were dressed up for, a birthday party? (Combing their hair, Mother had hissed through a mouthful of bobby-pins, "I want you to look your *best.*") They wore matching hair ribbons and carried little straw pocketbooks and when the tall nun with big feet opened the door they managed to smile anyway. In the black veil she looked like a great big tombstone; in spite of their terror they were polite.

"The Bidscombe girls," Sister Irmgarde said crossly. "You are much too late. And look at this," she said, jerking at the shoulders of Nelly's dress; she had a funny accent. "Your mama should take better care of you."

The girls were polite, they were! Nell thinks they curtseyed when all they wanted to do was run away from this huge, forbidding person. Nell knows they smiled. Why wouldn't she smile back? She wonders if it was against the rules of the order.

"You are too late for dinner," Sister Irmgarde said. "It is all put up. Wait here. I will fetch Mother Ludmilla. She has been waiting for you."

The little girls made as if to follow her. "No," she said, going through a door with a grate like the peephole on a speakeasy. "You cannot follow into the cloister."

Jake hissed, "She's scared we'll find out they're all spies."

"What's a cloister?"

"Shh, Nelly, be careful what you say. These people are foreigners."

The Johannines were a German order; when Mother Ludmilla came into the visitors' room she told them their father was a hero and they were very brave little girls, which confused Nelly and made Jake almost cry, and was the next to last thing she ever said to them. After that they fell into the hands of Sister Elsa, who was in charge of the younger children, and who whisked them out of their party dresses and into muslin nightgowns with a minimum of conversation.

"Now," she said, leading them into the darkened dormitory where a dozen other little girls squirmed in tangled bed sheets, "You will sleep here and here. Do not disturb the others."

As soon as she left, Nell crept into her sister's bed. "Why does she talk funny?"

"They all talk funny. They're Germans."

"I want to go home."

Agonized, Jake whispered, "We can't go home, I think we've been captured by the Nazis."

The Nazis! Hitler. He was almost as bad as Hirohito. Nelly hissed, "Oh no. Mother would never give us to the Nazis."

"Shh," Jake said as Nelly began weeping. "She doesn't know. They're pretending to be American. Don't cry. Oh please be quiet."

Nelly sobbed, "I can't."

At the far end of the dormitory a door opened on a black tombstone shape, framed in light, and Jake shoved Kolie into Nelly's mouth and held him there until Sister went away again. Thus protected from making any noise, Nelly bawled and bawled until finally Jake said:

"You have to shut up. Shut up and I'll draw the Red Line for you."

When in adult life Nelly charged her with this, too, Mother complained of the lengths she'd gone to, to get them in, the sacrifices she'd made to keep them there, the extra hours she'd had to work to meet the terrible expense. She made it clear Mariagaard was an exclusive school; they were honored to be allowed to go there.

It was like being in a prison camp. They were uniformed: navy jumpers for the girls, vests for the boys. They lived by rote.

There were unexplained acts of violence: girls' ears boxed, children slapped on the head with the Latin book—Sister Perpetua; boys switched for talking back—Sister Frederika. Once while they were playing in the beaten dirt outside, Sister Ursula swooped down and plucked one of the boys out of the group like a hawk seizing the weak puppy from a litter. From the playground the children could hear the *thwack* of the paddle and, through the open window of Mother Irmgarde's office, his shouts of pain.

There were rules, an order of march, regulations that made no sense to anybody but the nuns, who insisted on muslin nightgowns folded just *so*, tin cups put in *this* relationship to the enameled plates, children sitting at the trestle tables with their shoulders squared *thus* and a rap on the head with stony knuckles for the girl or boy who tired or forgot and began to sag.

Once Jake had to stand on her chair all through dinner and the evening because she'd whispered to Nelly during grace, and the food! Hot potato salad; potato pancakes; potato dumplings; rank meat on Sundays, disguised in stew. Mother Ludmilla made little sermons about food being sent overseas to our troops— whose?—shortages due to the war.

They ate boiled potatoes and lima beans in silence because some child—Jake?—had complained about the food.

Nell remembered pretty food on the table in the bungalow on Koolhawe Drive and Daddy singing at supper while Mother laughed and tried to shush him: yip yip yip. Shh, Dave, the neighbors. But in Washington Mother only opened cans for them and now they were here. She wedged her tongue in the floor of her mouth so she wouldn't cry.

Days marched with military precision; there was no leeway for laughter and except in chapel, no latitude for song; already Jake had spent three days condemned to silence for whispering in class; she was not allowed to talk, even in bed; Nelly had to make up her own story about the Red Line. Some sisters believed in sarcasm and psychological punishment. Others hit and yelled.

Nell was afraid of the rules but even more of breaking them; she was scared of these big people—women?—who moved like bears in spite of the starched guimpes and habits she later learned were patterned after the clothes worn by medieval saints. She was afraid for fractious Jake. Sister Elsa had given Jacqueline one more Last Warning. If she ignored it . . . Nell trembled. What would happen to them then?

In classes as at meals the sisters in their big shoes patrolled the aisles like prison guards, with habits held together by great, creaking leather belts from which their rosaries swung like instruments not of prayer but of retribution. The sisters uniformly used switches or, when pressed, threw erasers, but there were persistent rumors of stranglings and beatings with rosaries, children's backs scored with blood blisters in the shape of the rosary.

Although they taught and gave orders in English, the sisters spoke German among themselves, poor homesick women—no, poor girls, Nell thinks, separated from a mother country that was at war. Nell wonders now: *what must they have felt?* Stranded in America, they could have felt as persecuted, as pressed and sorely outnumbered as the children. And the war: how did they feel about it really, embarrassed or guilty or mortally sad? Miserable, Nell thinks now. Torn?

But at the time they stood for everything bad. When they gargled that foreign language, who knew what they were saying to each other? That they were fattening the girls for *Der Führer?* That in spite of the patriotic speeches after the newscast at the dinner hour, they really wanted the Nazis to win? If they weren't Nazis they were definitely Fifth Columnists. And when the Nazi planes landed or Nazi spies came ashore from their submarines and sneaked into the convent, what would happen to the children then? Nelly thought she and Jake ought to break into Mother Irmgarde's office and phone the police, or President Roosevelt. They had to make Mother take them away before something awful happened to them. As Nelly's night fears intensified, the Red Line got harder to draw and impossible to cross; Nelly couldn't do it alone, and Jake—Jake wouldn't play.

In October one of the big girls began bleeding mysteriously; all she did was pump too high on one of the swings. Blood got all over everything. Nell and Jake were horrified. Were the nuns doing tortures they didn't know about? Mother Irmgarde herself came out and took the big girl off the playground, shaking her shoulders and scolding in a fierce undertone.

The girl began to wail and Nelly wailed.

The blood. The shame.

Nell could not stop crying even when Jake tried to shush her. Terrified, she heard her own voice twining up and up in a stringy, apparently unending scream.

"Shh, Nelly." Jake was scowling, worried. "They're coming."

But her throat was wide open now; sound kept coming out.

"Stop it or they'll hit you," Jake hissed.

Then Sister Elsa had her by the shoulders, shaking, shaking. "Stop that."

"I can't help it." Nelly sobbed. Behind or around them other children were milling, whimpering, the mass ready to fly apart in a million particles.

"She can't help it," Jake cried protectively.

"Stop. Now," Sister Elsa cried, looking at the girls, the others: encroaching hysteria. Did they detect a false note, a certain lack of conviction? Uncertainty? "Quiet."

"The blood." Nelly's voice went on streaming out, "The blood, the blood."

"The blood. It is nothing, chust nature," Sister Elsa was mortified, "you. . . . "

"The blood!"

Desperate, Sister Elsa kept shaking her; "You have to stop."

Jake shouted, "Don't you hurt my sister."

"Stop it." Sister's face crumpled; it was as if she herself were in pain; in her chagrin her verbal powers slipped as she shook the stiff and wailing Nelly, trying to bring her back to life as they knew it. "Oh blease, Nellanor. Blease."

"Let go," Jake screamed, and flew into the nun's midsection; perhaps like Nell she was afraid Sister could do something that made them bleed too. Desperate, she pummeled Nell's captor until both she and Sister Elsa were horrified; Sister began to cry. Everything stopped at once. "You let her go," Jake finished, breathing hard.

"Chust stop." Weeping, Sister Elsa let go. "Oh, blease." She would have let them do anything: eat ice cream, skip class. What they did do was retreat to Jake's bed even though it was midafternoon and they weren't allowed in the dormitory until after study hall.

"That's it," Jake said. "The end."

Nelly swallowed air. "What are we going to do?"

"I don't know."

"Run away?"

"So they can shoot at us?"

"Behind the Red Line."

"Don't be a baby." Spinning on the end of the bed in the navy serge jumper, Jacqueline was daring, brilliant. "Just wait. I'm getting us out."

"Where are you going?"

"Chapel. You'll see."

The chapel: it was lovely, Nell sees now—miniature Gothic altar carved of marble with a statue of the Virgin on the right so beautifully wrought that it outshone the figure on the crucifix. Jacqueline stayed there through the dinner bell; there was a flurry when Sister noticed her empty seat. Sister Ludmilla was dispatched to get her. She returned frustrated, confused, buzzing to Mother Irmgarde who looked stern but did not speak.

When they went to chapel for night prayers Jake was still kneeling in front of the statue of the Virgin, stiff as a little icon with her back straight in the serge jumper; when one by one the sisters went up to whisper to Jacqueline, she did not recognize them and she did not respond; instead she knelt as if transfixed, and when the others filed out at bedtime and Mother Irmgarde tugged, expecting her to join them, Jake listed slightly with the superior's weight but did not stir.

At bedtime Jake was still there, and something about the fact that she was making her stand in the chapel—sanctuary?—kept the sisters from removing her by force.

In the dormitory the other little girls whispered and giggled long after lights out. The rigid lock step of their lives at Mariagaard had been broken. Sister Elsa patrolled the aisles looking pressed, distraught; at her back she must have heard intimations of insurgency and beyond it the roar of impending chaos. If Jake could do this and get away with it, anything could happen. The children could rise up and lash her down like Gulliver. The police could come and arrest her as a German spy.

The next morning Sister Elsa came in before the rising bell to get Nelly. Stuffing their things back into suitcases, hustling Nell downstairs in the early light, Sister was forlorn and weepy; at Mother Irmgarde's door she snuffled, murmuring, "Perhaps you will tell them I tried to take care of you." She released Nelly with a prickly little hug.

Even Mother Irmgarde was upset this morning, but Jake. Tired as she was, with her face white and smeared from a whole night of not sleeping, she was triumphant. Jake waved at her from behind Mother Irmgarde's back with a savage little grin. "You," the superior said; her face was stiff with suppressed tears; "We tried to help you. This. It is so sad."

In the taxi going back down the long drive to the road that led back up the Eastern Shore to Washington, fierce little Jacqueline said, "What I did was, I had a vision. I told them the Blessed Mother came down in a cloud and said we had to go home to Honolulu."

For Nell, this is an abstraction. "You mean the statue?"

"The vision," Jake said and to this day Nell can't be sure whether or not it was an invention: those eyes. Crackling like cinders, with the whites showing all the way around. "They got afraid. They didn't know if I was having it or not."

And Mother: what fears had Jake raised in her, in all of them? When she came down to the curb to meet them, Mother was wispy and distracted; she too had been crying. "Oh, what am I going to do with you now?" she said in combined bitterness and remorse and—yes, resentment, Nell realizes, because her sister's passion had thrust Mother's needy little girls back between her and the purity of her grieving. "Oh, God. I only wanted what was best for you."

Only now is Nell able to come to terms with this; with her mouth flooding, she says, "Oh, poor Mother!"

"Shh," Jake says and with a bravery that moves both of them strokes her sister's forehead.

With the uncomfortable, doggedly loyal Jake *this close,* Nell is finally able to say, "The Red Line."

"Yes." Understanding now, Jake knows what to do. Without having to be told, she pulls it up through the years to now in the same old incantatory tone, drawing it from memory. "The Red Line cuts through the darkness and sometimes we see it."

Nell says, "And sometimes we go across."

Jake says gently, "You want me to try and take you across?"

"Not really." Holding her breath against pain Nell feels temporary release and expels it: *pah.* "I need to see." The Red Line? The vision? Does she hope for illumination or release? She is not sure; she says, "I only want to see what you saw."

Jake takes her hand; she may or may not know what Nell is talking about. She loves Nell; she'll say anything. "You're going to lick this thing," she says.

Nell may lick it, for the time being at least; perhaps she can; she does not know. What she does know is that if she can only concentrate on this one thing and hold it tight, she may be able to understand it: that this intangible—what? Whatever it is, it came before the beginning and cuts through and perhaps outweighs considerations of survival. It is this that she and her sister shared in Honolulu and at Mariagaard and it is this that she sees shimmering in the room between them—the prevailing, ameliorating factor, the potential—the fragile but pervasive presence of the supernatural, here as before suggested or expressed in the persistence of love.

—Amelia Manning's story

Thief of Lives

We are wedged in the car again, heading for another week-end at the Warriners', with everybody but me going along in more or less happy expectation. Families in collision at this year's summer place, the ex-farmhouse with the cracked ironstone and absent strangers' treasures drying in the backs of dresser drawers. My heart sinks as we cross the state line; should I have thrown in the quartz heater? This time am I going to know which vines it's safe to touch? Dave and the children make fun of my imagination of disaster; once burned, I resent their chronic calm. The country is crawling with poison ivy. These places are always dank. At best we're going to be uncomfortable. I wish we had brought the dog.

I say morosely, "First Stan's going to say, 'Did you have any trouble finding us?' And you're going to say, 'No, your directions were very good.'"

"I thought you liked the Warriners."

A head bobs up behind me. "Mom."

"I like Sue," I say. "I like the kids." I like my own house and my security corner; I like my pet fork; I even like Stan Warriner except when we are alone in tight places, which makes me squirm. Hard to explain what depresses me. Ravens fly up at the crossroads squalling *Turn back, turn back.*

"Mom."

Years of practice have taught us how to float conversation in spite of incursions; Dave says, "Then you're going to say, 'Oh Sue, how did you ever find this place?' and she'll hug you and say, 'Just lucky, I guess.'"

"Yes, she will." It's part of this very complicated package we keep unwrapping: my need for her regard.

"Mo-om."

I wheel on my youngest, whose mouth is smeared with some candy I don't even know the name of. "I know, I know, his arm is on your side of the back seat, so shut up."

His brother sees my exposed flank and strikes. "Grandmother says never say shut up."

"Well do me a favor and shut up anyway."

"Are we almost there?"

"Shut up, we're almost there."

Dave says, "If you hate these weekends, we don't have to come."

"Oh give me a break," I say.

Back in New London I used to take the long way home from school when I was little, trailing my backpack through hedges along the road to Ocean Beach. Orphaned by an accident at sea, I wasn't ready to recognize the fact. Missing in Action was as much as I could handle at the time; my father might be coming back! In the winter I slouched outside other people's houses waiting for the lights to go on because I needed to watch families. I had to see them sitting down to eat. Never mind if the dad happened to look out and see something moving in the black twilight under his dining room window: only some kid. If my mother dropped lumpy creamed tuna on damp toast at night and could not stop running to the window because the wreck of the *Thresher* had beggared us, no matter. I knew how things were supposed to be done. All life went on inside those windows with me safe in the bushes beating time, yeah yeah, yearning after their food. It was like TV.

When I got bored I could turn it off.

See how it is? We can always go home. Riding to the War-riners' I sit on my heel, squirming in combined guilt and anticipation because I am stripping to go skinny-dipping in their lives. I love that they want to see us but forgive me, it's a disease: I can't shut off the camera that records, and no matter how close we think we are, I can't snaffle the part that keeps running ahead to judge.

Every summer they show us around the worst places, proud as the prince and princess of Monaco: it isn't much but we like it. You mean this is where we *sleep?* Stan likes to get finished in the bathroom first, so if you guys wouldn't mind. . . . No matter how nice they are, when you go into other people's houses you become a stateless person, subject to their timetable and bound by their rules. Why do we fold ourselves into the car and persist? Who wants to travel great distances just to spend the nights in iron cots wedged under the gable in some summer place where raw boards carry every sound, and do we really need to sit down to eat knowing that afterward our captors are going to have a fight about whose turn it is to wash up?

Two things. One. It's not what you're doing but what you *think* you're doing that makes the difference. For a long time Dave and I thought we and the Warriners were trying to do all the same things—that they were the only two people who cared as much as we did about family. Like us, they used to go home early from parties to hang out with their kids. Like us, they made celebrations, Saturday afternoon movies with the kids and the big brunch on Sundays after church. Walk into our houses on any weekend and you'd find us sitting down to Sunday night supper at the same time, heads bent over the table: ceremony. Sue and I used to meet in the late afternoons when we both had babies and before they moved; we used to do each other's hair, and if her taste is not my taste, if her anger sometimes surprises me, if she sulks until Stan begs her to tell him what's the matter, these seem like small differences.

And the other: where I used to plaster myself to all those lighted windows I am rich now—jumbled household, noisy family. I need to let the people see me. I need to see them.

Listen, these are our best friends from the great bonding period of early marriage. We used to play Scrabble and eat M&Ms at each other's houses and put our first babies down to sleep in the same crib. How could we tell them we don't want to come?

Approaching the sagging farmhouse, Dave says to me, "Speak, in the name of heaven."

"I miss the dog."

We open the car doors and release the kids. In the magical way of these weekends, my two see Sue's three playing outside this year's barn and zot, five children disappear. We won't see them again until it's time to eat. Which is the third thing. In the absence of extended family, we give our sons extended friends.

We've even signed joint papers. If anything happens to us the Warriners will take the children and do the same by them as we would. At least I think they will.

"Yutch," my oldest says, "Mr. Warriner's growing a beard."

Outward and physical manifestation of an inner and spiritual—What? "Shh. Go find the kids."

The Warriners have come down to meet us and in this light it's hard to see their faces, matronly Sue with her sweater riding up over the denim wraparound and saturnine Stan, who is oddly disheveled; you'd think that having more money would make people be happy and look sharp—stop me before I kill again, why can't I just *enjoy* them? For all his needling Stan is steady and loyal, loyal; he can be counted on to come out in the night if you need him to bring your backup door key or babysit one of your children while you take the other to the emergency room. Sue drops one-liners with that great unexpected giggle. Loving Sue, good Stan.

Gulp. We are in their territory now. But if they make the rules, formula dictates the timetable: Friday night supper's on the stove and after the usual tour of the premises we will sit down to eat. Saturday all four of us will sleep as late as the kids will let us and count on it, we'll have hot dogs for lunch. Then we will go see the beaver dam, natural falls, antique dealer, whatever is the local attraction, after which we'll buy whatever's in season, strawberries in June, corn in August, our contribution to dinner that night. While Stan and Dave take the kids off somewhere, Sue and I will spend a long time cooking, which is part of the entertainment on these weekends; Sunday we'll leave in time to get home before dark but not so early that it looks like an escape. Another reason we come is because going home is so sweet.

We are protected by the order of march.

Stan says, "Did you have any trouble getting here?"

And this time I'm the one who says, "No, your directions were very good."

I know Dave is laughing as he says my line. "Oh Sue, how did you ever find this place?"

Surprise, this time she hugs him instead of me. "Just lucky, I guess." Over his shoulder I see tears standing in her eyes. Her face is altered by the thirty pounds she's put on and I entertain the fear that she's changed or is about to begin changing in some stunning act of disloyalty to our past.

Stan says, "Wait until you see my asparagus."

Sue catches me looking at her and drops her arms. "Let me show you where you're going to sleep."

In the constricted guest room with bare board walls my friend turns back the beds with the sweetest Princess Grace smile, but her fingers are stained yellow because she's begun smoking again and to compensate for the stains she's using nail polish. Even though it's just us, Sue has done full makeup, with eyeliner arching over the top curve of her eyelids and iridescent shadow so thick you can see the outline of the pupils when she closes them. She's spent a lot on her sweater, one of those hand-knitted numbers with the rosebud pattern and— lord, I think she's wearing a girdle. Oh Sue I miss you when you were thin.

I note that the bedroom partitions only go part of the way up. It's OK for two nights, but she and Stan are here for the whole summer, chockablock with three prurient, wakeful preadolescent sons.

"It doesn't matter," she says even though I haven't spoken, "nothing's happening anyway."

"Oh, Sue!" Guiltily I think: Tell me, and then quickly: No, don't tell me. We already know things are not wonderful between the Warriners because of the presents they give each other; last Christmas she gave him a copy of the *OED* with magnifying glass and he gave her a set of snow tires. Once they went in together on driveway sealer for the house. I want to take Sue by the shoulders and beg her to stay the same, but she's helped me put the L. L. Bean bags into what passes for a closet and it's time for me to fish out the house present—Rhine wine this time, along with smoked salmon from the neighborhood fish store. When I give her the extra package, a violet scarf I picked up because I know she loves the color, she thanks me in a shaky little voice and all the time I am remembering that on these weekends we used to be able to look at each other without complications. If my mind is running fast-forward, envisioning disaster, that's my problem; my friend whose waist has disappeared into the rest of her has pulled the scarf in front of her face like a *bourka* and we are both laughing.

She says, "Even the mailman has started looking good to me."

The *Thresher.* At first they only said there had been an accident at sea and everybody was being rescued. Then they only said he was missing. It took seven years for them to come right out and tell me and my mother that my father was dead, by which time I had imagined him coming home in a thousand different scenarios.

Once you know this is the way things are in the world you will think anything you have to, for protection. I want to beg Sue to be careful. I say, "You would never do that."

Under her eye makeup the shadows go around and around and around. "There's no telling what I will do."

I am struck by something one of my kids told me: "Stanny says his mom isn't anything like you think when we're not here." Without us present, ebullient Sue turns into something else. Remember, we used to think we were all trying to do the same things.

At least dinner is the same: Sue's bean soup and homemade bread along with ruby lettuce from Stan's garden and Dave's Rhine wine, all nine of us, parents and kids sitting down with our heads bent over the table while Stan says grace—unself-conscious, pretty, usual. Sue had spun out the afternoon's wait by having her three make sugar cookies as big as cartwheels ("Are they here yet?" "Shh, help your brother shake the jimmies on."), and while Stan grinned in a delighted, proprietary way she brought out ice cream made from Georgia peaches trucked into the Eagle market right down in the middle of this country town and cream from the local dairy, look over the back fence and you can see the cows. Bringing back a rural past that was dead long before we discovered the country, Sue did the finishing work right at the table, spinning the dasher a few more times in the freezing mush.

Listen, this is why we come. Together like this, by candlelight under exposed beams that glow in reflected firelight, we are creating not ceremony so much as a semblance, and if this is the best we can manage, well maybe OK fine. Maybe this is the best there is.

Then after dinner the five kids pulled us out to the barn to watch them put on costumes and lip-synch *Annie* one more time while we perched on a bench and Stan put that proprietary arm around Sue: My sweet girl. In the glow from massed flash-lights and three kerosene lanterns I could look at my old friends' softening faces and think we were still the same. Going back up to the house Dave hangs back and when I dawdle so I can walk with him he mutters, "Stan has some kind of bee up his ass."

"Oh shit." It's not TV. No, maybe it is; that disconcerting, guilty flicker. In the absence of an ice cave or spectacular natural falls, we will watch the Warriners fight. "What?"

But there is a little kid bopping along behind us in the darkness, either one of ours or one of theirs and this is another thing: our kids have the same tufted brown hair and good square heads and three out of five wear the same kind of tortoiseshell glasses; they're all of a piece. "Later," Dave says.

It goes without saying. We will hash this over at length when we get home, but one of the rules of the weekend territory is that you never talk about your hosts or guests while you are on the same premises, and you can second-guess but you must never, ever gloat.

In bed that night, listening to the people in the house settling around us, sleepless Stan Warriner sighing in the living room while Sue dreams and in the loft our children huffle and squeak like small animals, Dave and I manage to wedge ourselves into one of the cots, where we embrace in the savage guilt of the survivor. The true pleasure the Warriners give us is never in the farmhouse visit or the dinner or the brandy Stan brings out afterward but in the nature of the company. It is in the persistence of contrasts: not it. Not that way. Not Dave. Not me.

But in the morning it is as if none of this has happened; smirched by whisker burn, I join Sue over the breakfast dishes and think guilty thoughts. Her butt spreads under the big chenille robe today and she says, "So I had to give up aerobics classes because I got too busy, I'm teaching two extra English classes because I'm going to need the money." She waits for me to ask the question and when I don't she says, without explaining, "I'm getting some things in my life straightened out."

Maybe I am a bad friend. I say foolishly, "Maybe you guys should go for some counseling."

When Sue turns, her blue eyes are so bland and empty that I can almost see through to the back of her head. "Why would I want to do that?" she says.

Let me tell you something about the imagination of disaster. One mishap, one slip where trouble catches you not looking, and you will have it whether or not you want it; like it or not you will run ahead of the imagination of disaster for the rest of your life and even in your best moments, you're aggressively forearmed.

Yet when we pile into our Wagoneer with all five kids bouncing in the back-back and head off for the Eagle market to score a goose—Sue's idea for the big Saturday night dinner—it's as before.

Even better, we begin riffing in counterpoint: "What's that color you're wearing, it's very becoming" / "Becoming what?" /

"Becoming a public nuisance" / "Conduct unbecoming . . ." happy, nothing chatter, I am grateful. I count on certain things, like the consistency of our past, and if goose in August seems a little unlikely, I think, Fine.

Later Sue will tell me, "We were never what you thought we were," but that is in the future and at the moment we're rattling along in the Wagoneer, gnawing apricot leather from the general store and paddling in the summer light.

While the goose roasts, Sue starts with Stan about the bizarre blend of bourbon and Bailey's which he's taken to drinking when the shadows start collecting in the late afternoon, and accidentally I walk in on him telling her it's so fucking cold around here that he's got to get warm any way he can, which is both alarming and wonderful. Lord, do I get off on the contrast between Stan and Sue and the two of us? Listen, surviving the wreck of the *Thresher* I am as giddy as Lazarus with the tables turned, sitting down at my own banquet and throwing heavily frosted chunks of cake: take that you guys, whoever. And that. And that and that and that. It becomes important for me to scour the sink and shuck corn and cream the butter for Sue's cranberry bread; I even grease the tins. I will do anything for her, to make up.

Dave is off at the pond with the kids, creating a diversion so we can get this major feast on the table, and when he comes back into the kitchen he seems surprised to find dripping Sue conducting all her conversations with Stan through me: "Jenny, see whether Stan wants to make the orange sauce or whether he wants me to do it." Then, "Jenny, it's time for Stan to go down to the garden and bring up the lettuce." She adds carelessly, "You can go help him if you want." The last thing I want is to be alone in the garden at twilight with needy Stan.

The kids come in marching behind Dave, who's done one of his best numbers, playing imaginary drill sergeant, whatever— scout leader, logging chief—the little boys are all walking tall, like woodsmen in jackboots: Watch out, I take large steps.

They pile up in the doorway as Dave assesses the situation and says to Stan, "Come on, guy. Garden. I'll help." When we reconsider this moment in the inevitable instant replay, he isn't going to be able to point to anything Stan said to him out there in the garden that would prepare us for what happens next.

We are sitting down at the trestle table like good pilgrims, waiting for Stan to cut into the goose. It is so pretty! This unseasonal feast has made the kitchen so hot that we sit with the back door open, looking out over the set table at the expanse of grass leading away to the garden, at this summer's geraniums in perky pots bordering the walk. Sue has brought out homemade cranberry bread and corn and boiled potatoes and with an unnecessary flourish she's put on my oyster dressing and the sweet potato casserole; these Saturday night feasts in the country used to be simple, but as things have changed Sue has found it necessary to put on more and more dog. Therefore we're sitting there in August looking at all that food while our host addresses the goose with his shirtsleeves pushed high and the sweat rolling down, everything more or less pleasant until Stan makes the first cut and meets a little bit too much resistance and begins to saw until the tendons grab his blade. Frustrated, he tries another cut and his knife bounces off, at which point he slaps the top of the rubbery bird with his bare fist making fat fly. His voice is big and angry:

"Son of a bitch, this thing isn't cooked."

Sue forgets and says to him directly, "Of course it is."

"The hell." He is personally affronted. "Look at it. There's blood coming out."

"No there isn't."

"You're going to have to put it back."

"It looks fine to me."

He lifts the thing a few inches and bounces it on the platter. "I said, put it back."

Never mind her tears. "I can't put it back, everything's all ready."

Dave and I are afraid to exchange looks. I'm sitting on my heel. Their voices go on, sharp and soft, sharp and soft.

"Well you can't serve it this way."

"If we wait, dinner will be wrecked."

"Dinner's already wrecked."

Dave says mildly, "No problem, we can wait."

Sue mourns. "Everything was going to be so nice."

I suggest that we can eat the trimmings while we're waiting but nobody hears. The Warriners are sawing back and forth.

"I'd rather eat dogshit," Stan says in a rage so huge that the kids, who might have laughed, are afraid to laugh.

"You." In a voice I don't recognize, Sue says the unforgivable. "Why do you always have to ruin everything?" Understands what she's done; her hands fly into her mouth. "Oh, Stan!"

Too late. With a terrifying laugh Stan has picked up the bird and as we watch he hurls it down and drop kicks it out the open kitchen door. Then he grabs the loaf of cranberry bread and with a feral look goes outside, kicking the door shut behind him. We can hear a motor start.

Weeping, Sue sits in the rubble of her dinner, graciously serving us gravy on potatoes, both kinds, and tomorrow morning's blueberry muffins and corn and more corn while her eldest, with an accustomed calm, breaks out sausage and a package of chipped beef and copes. I imagine Stan crouched on the rocks at the beaver dam, gnawing the cranberry loaf; maybe it's the contrast that makes what we have here taste so good. By the time we reach dessert, a Christmas pudding Sue's saved until she had enough people present to finish it, we sound borderline festive; the kids forget, and laugh.

Alone in the kitchen with my friend Sue, addressing the dishes, I try to create the kind of silence into which confidences will fall but she isn't talking. Instead she surprises me.

I say, "You must be kind of pissed at us."

Those blank eyes turn on me: "Why would I be pissed at you?"

"Well, if we hadn't come. . . ."

"It would have been something else," she says. But when Sue looks at me this time she catches me out: the sightseer who can go home after she's seen the beaver dam. "I suppose you think this is all very funny," she says.

"That's the last thing I think."

Without aiming, Sue hits me dead center. "I see you watching. I know what you think."

When the *Thresher* sank the worst thing I felt, forgive me, was the misery of being turned into something different. I could hardly forgive my mother for what she did to us because I knew the whole thing was a result of her carelessness—losing my father like that, just letting him go! Just try and prove to other kids that you're not an orphan, that you're just the same as everybody else. I am looking at Sue. "I think these things blow up and then they blow away," I say carefully, because I am intent on protecting all of us.

"Don't think you know what goes on with us."

"Dave and I have our fights too."

Her voice shakes with anger. "Don't even pretend you think you know."

I am surprised into anger too. "If we're such a big problem for you, why do you keep on having us?"

Tears fill her eyes but she just shakes her head.

Considering her grief I think coldly of what my friend Iris said in quite another context: *Everything serves somebody's purposes.* Stricken, I fall back three steps and look at myself.

I am Lazarus, revived and blossoming; after all that with the *Thresher* I am disproportionately rich. No more running to the window, everybody I care about is safe at home. Worse, I know that when I am done looking at this life of Sue's I can just turn it off, like bad TV.

I'm voyeur, or is it voyeuse, guilty as sin and saying, in a faulty attempt to make up for it, "Maybe it would be a good idea if Dave and I got the kids together and went back tonight. Before it gets too late, I mean." I really mean: before Stan gets back and they have another fight.

And in an astonishing act of understanding and forgiveness, my sweet friend lifts her hands to hold me in place. "Oh no," she says. This is how we approach the truth of it, Sue saying brightly, "We're going to take you swimming, and Stan hasn't showed you the new path he's working on, with leftover bricks?"

I am ashamed. "I just thought maybe we ought to. . . ."

"We love having you here."

Right, Iris, everything that persists really does serve some-body's purposes. My aunt and uncle, who once solemnly told me that there were more important things in life than having children, used to talk to each other through their dogs. They had matched Scotties, MacLady and MacFluff. "Tell Daddy you want your collar tighter." "Oh look, adorable." "Oh Sal, look at MacLady's ears!" Without the dogs my aunt and uncle were like the tree in the lost forest, falling with nobody to hear. The dogs were their vehicles for expression. Now the Warriners had dogs, had children, but in that weekend it became clear that in the lexicon of sealed marriages as mysterious as the crypt that no explorer can presume to look into, or understand, their vehicle for expression was us.

We went home on Sunday after a pretty good day with the Warriners, in which Stan made sourdough pancakes to make up for the disruption and Sue boiled fresh blueberries and sugar into a syrup, with sunlight melting the butter on the farmer's willowware. There was a flea market; the faded quilts and spunky salt-and-peppers selling for pennies left me a little de-pressed. Somebody had set up a ferris wheel on the drive-in parking lot and Stan and Dave took the kids for rides while Sue tried on and bought a vintage blouse from the twenties studded with crystal and jet; if she is dressing according to her expecta-tions, then things can't be so bad.

We left early enough to make it home before dark but not so early that it looked like an escape, Dave and me thoughtful, our boys raucous with relief. I think my sons were in the back play-ing Married Couple: "Oh, you don't like the turkey?" Bop. At home we would make them a celebration, pizza and fudge and TV, so while all about them were losing theirs they would know incontrovertibly that at least we were all right.

It's late, and Dave and I will save everything we have to say until we're home and the kids are fed and washed and kissed good night and stashed. They lie under the covers with an amaz-ingly smug look that I recognize. None of that dumb fighting stuff around here, right Mom? But this is later. Riding away I flash on our old friends standing in the driveway with their kids tumbling behind them—good Sue, who in spite of the added weight is surprisingly pretty, and I think, Oh God I love you guys. And the part of me that runs along ahead catches its foot in something and snags. Oh God, guys. Please take care of yourselves.